PEACE IN THE MOUNTAIN HAVEN

CALL OF THE ROCKIES ~ BOOK 7

MISTY M. BELLER

Misty M. Beller
BOOKS

ISBN-13 Trade Paperback: 978-1-954810-26-6

ISBN-13 Large Print Paperback: 978-1-954810-27-3

ISBN-13 Casebound Hardback: 978-1-954810-28-0

To my own sweet Haven.
You are a delight and so talented.
Never forget how much I love you.

Thy mercy, O Lord, is in the heavens; and thy faithfulness reacheth unto the clouds.

Thy righteousness is like the great mountains; thy judgments are a great deep: O Lord, thou preservest man and beast.

How excellent is thy lovingkindness, O God! therefore the children of men put their trust under the shadow of thy wings.

.

Psalm 36:5-7 (KJV)

CHAPTER 1

*I*t was time to leave.

Watkuese stared across the grassland, her gaze hovering on the two children playing, then rising to focus on the mountains beyond. She'd planned to return across those peaks to her village long before now, but lingering among these friends had become so comfortable. The way they gathered around her like family, easing the load she'd been bearing without even realizing until its weight had lightened. If she only had herself to think of, she might be tempted to stay in this place through the colder months. After that...she could come and go when she pleased.

But she no longer had the luxury of only considering herself. She had a daughter to raise, one entrusted to her not through birth, but through loss. A loss they'd both felt in their deepest beings.

Her daughter hadn't found the healing they'd been hoping

1

for here. Instead, Pop-pank's difficulties had intensified, her sullen attitudes and the way she pulled away more each day.

Watkuese's life had never felt so out of control than with this child, this daughter of her heart. They had to leave...before something happened that was too awful to fix.

Two small figures scampering across the grassland captured her focus, and her chest tightened as she studied them. Pop-pank led the way, and River Boy, her cousin's son, toddled behind, doing his best to keep up on his stubby legs. Pop-pank's six winters had made her lean and willowy, so much like her mother's lithe form.

Where was Pop-pank leading the lad this time? The cousins loved to play together, despite the four winters separating their ages. But was her daughter a bad influence on the innocent lad? More and more often, she would sneak him away to hide in the underbrush, ignoring all the worried calls of people searching for them. Or when someone took them into the trees to pick berries and chokecherries, Pop-pank alone would disappear up a tree or down a ravine, tucked beneath a rock.

Why did the girl take such pleasure in hiding while the adults searched frantically? During every search, as Watkuese's desperation surged, the images of what might happen to her daughter nearly brought her to her knees, stealing her breath, choking her with panic.

If she failed her dearest friend—didn't keep that final desperate promise before Kimana's life slipped away... No, she couldn't let that happen. Even more, she couldn't bear the thought of losing the daughter she never expected to have, who now meant everything to her.

The two children neared the end of the area where she allowed them to play, and Watkuese cupped her hands around her mouth to call for them. Before she could make a sound, a figure leaped from the trees, scattering the shrieking children and sending Watkuese's heart into her throat.

She charged forward, but recognition struck after her first step.

Louis? One of Colette's brothers—the younger. He still acted a bit like a lad himself, yet he'd grown so tall and muscular, on the cusp of becoming a warrior. He must be coming back with some of the other men from the hunt. The children recognized him too and turned, running toward him now, still giggling loud enough to scare away game for a great distance.

Louis clutched his head and gave a dramatic show of falling to his knees, then twisting to lie on his back in the grass. River Boy dove on him, and Pop-pank knelt at the man's side as they engulfed him in tickles.

The merry sounds echoing across the open land would make anyone smile, including the three men who'd stepped from the woods after Louis's dramatic entrance. Adam and Joel, brothers among this group of friends, stood side by side. A little apart from them, Louis's brother Hugh seemed separate, as he had so often in the months she'd stayed here.

He was a mystery, that one. A loner, even though the group often tried to pull him in. He would answer questions and even added to conversations, and he always took part in the hunting and any other work the village braves were assigned. But he kept his distance.

That round scar on his temple hinted at an interesting story. And something deep hung in his eyes, a weight that restrained him. What happened in his past to lay such a heavy burden on him?

Louis was so lighthearted. Hugh carried enough load for both brothers.

The man hovering in her thoughts lifted his gaze, meeting hers as though he'd known she'd been watching. She should look away, as any respectable maiden would. But she'd never allowed others' expectations to control her. Nor was she ashamed to be caught studying this man.

Not just because he was a white man. He was intriguing in his own right, piquing her interest—something she'd not felt for a man in so long...maybe ever.

One more reason why she had to leave soon. Perhaps even tomorrow. Could she slip away in the night? That way she could avoid the long string of farewells—the sadness and pressure to stay.

She needed freedom. Needed to find a place that would soothe the craving inside her. And even more than that, she needed to find a way to help her daughter.

This night then. She and Pop-pank would be off, and together, they would find the place that truly settled their souls.

In the Shoshone village where she'd first met Pop-pank's parents, she'd come the closest to finding that peace, so they would start there. The sooner they reached that camp across the mountains, the better.

∾

*T*he call of the trail had grown so loud, Hugh Charpentier's entire body stirred with the clamor of it.

He crouched by the campfire in the fading daylight, adjusting the spit of rabbit meat to cook a different section. Finding decent game in this territory had become harder as the summer progressed. No wonder this quiet Nez Perce town ate mostly salmon and camas root.

The scuff of a moccasin alerted him to a man approaching from behind. Caleb Jackson stepped up to the circle of warmth from the fire, then eased down to sit on a rock. Hugh glanced his way with a nod.

Caleb returned the greeting. "Smells good."

Hugh scanned the meat. "There's plenty for you and your family. Just about ready too." There may not be enough to fill all their bellies, but perhaps Caleb's wife would volunteer baked camas cakes to round out the meal.

Caleb raised a hand, palm out. "I appreciate the thought, but Otskai's been cooking a stew that's had my mouth watering all afternoon. You're welcome to come by for a bowlful if you'd like." Though Caleb was white, his Nez Perce wife excelled at using all the local herbs and roots to season her food to perfection.

Hugh offered a tight smile but didn't speak. This meat would be plenty for him and Louis. Of course, his brother might well feast on the rabbit, then stop by Caleb's lodge to visit and end up eating the stew too. Louis seemed to thrive on interacting with others. And with the charm and easygoing nature he'd inherited from their mother, he was welcomed everywhere he went. Of the three brothers, Louis was the best of them.

Caleb had lapsed into silence, and Hugh glanced at him again. He would be happy to enjoy the quiet for hours, but Caleb didn't usually visit without a reason.

The man was watching him, his eyes scrutinizing in a way that made Hugh's neck itch. He held Caleb's gaze. Waited. He wasn't one to back down from a challenge or be pushed aside. Not that Caleb would provoke—the fellow was as laid back as his frame was large—but he clearly wanted something.

At last, the corner of his mouth tipped up, and the edges of his eyes crinkled. Not a full smile, but close. "I have a question for you, Hugh. I guess more of a request, really."

Hugh dipped his chin just enough to bid the man continue.

Caleb reached for a strip of bark and flicked scraps off as he spoke. "Louis mentioned the two of you might be headed out soon. Is that what you're still thinking?"

He had to bite back a frown. Why did Louis share their plans with people who didn't need to know them? He'd learn not to do that soon enough. The more you kept your distance from others, the easier it was to part ways.

Hugh had been taught the lesson the hard way, but he'd learned it well.

To Caleb, he offered a single nod.

"Well..." Caleb drew out the word, his focus falling to the bark as his brow furrowed. At last, he looked up and met Hugh's gaze again, his expression growing earnest. "Here's the thing. You know my wife's cousin, Watkuese, and her daughter?"

He waited long enough for Hugh to nod that he did. "Well, Otskai is pretty certain her cousin is ready to head back across the mountains to the Shoshone village where she was living before."

Hugh had no idea what this had to do with him, but once more, he nodded when Caleb paused.

"Watkuese has a habit of slipping away when no one expects and going it alone. Otskai thinks she's going to do that again this time, and that worries us. Especially with the weather getting colder and little Pop-pank with her."

Hugh raised his brows. With winter creeping in more every day, crossing the mountains would be hard for anyone, especially a woman and child traveling alone. He was developing an inkling of what this might have to do with him, and the idea stuck like porcupine quills in his chest. He held his tongue, though, and waited.

"We thought if you were headed across the mountains, too, maybe you and Louis would see Watkuese and her daughter to their village. It'd be a relief to know they're with someone capable of keeping them safe through any hardships."

The spikes in his chest turned to a searing burn. What in the heavens made Caleb think he would be the right person to coddle a woman and child across the Rocky Mountains? He wasn't good with people, especially females.

He tried to keep his voice casual enough to hide the roiling inside. "I don't know. Not sure I'm the right man for the job."

Caleb's brows rose. "You're very skilled when it comes to

traveling in the mountains. You've spent more time there than I have. And I know you'd take good care of them both. The fact that you came all the way from Rupert's Land to make sure Colette was settled tells me all I need to hear."

Hugh turned the rabbit again to keep from fiddling with his hands. "I owed it to her and the babe both. I should have made sure things were better with Raphael. That she wasn't bearing the brunt of..." His brother had been so much like their father, but Hugh had never seen signs of him drinking like Pa had. He should have known that the habit could start anytime. Should have kept better watch.

He pulled himself from the past, forcing his thoughts on Caleb's request as the man spoke again.

"Are you worried about leaving Colette and the baby? French is pretty smitten with them both. I think he'd go to the end of the earth to provide for them. Of course, we'll all help with anything they need."

Hugh had no doubt this group of friends would gather around Colette and her new husband and babe, should they need help. Though not actually connected by blood, these friends seemed like the kind of family anyone would want.

The kind he'd never fit into.

Hugh said none of that, though. "Louis and I were planning to head out for the winter trapping season. We'll be back to check on Colette and the babe, but I don't think she needs us so close anymore." Raphael would have loved his new daughter, though Hugh had a feeling he would have been just as clumsy holding the tiny bundle as Hugh was whenever he worked up the nerve to take her from Colette.

Caleb leaned forward, bracing his elbows on his knees. "So how about it? Will you see Watkuese back home? You would have our gratitude, and I'll gladly send a passel of furs along with you the next time you go to trade. You can keep all the profit."

Hugh eyed him. "Bribery isn't necessary." He could harvest enough furs to trade for what he and Louis needed.

The thought of being responsible for a woman and child he barely knew made his belly churn. But could he really say no? Allow her to slip away and fend for herself on that treacherous journey?

And the child. Six years old, the same age Louis had been when they'd had to leave the Heinrichs' farm. Sent back home to face life with Pa. Louis had been so young and innocent, so vulnerable. As much as Hugh had wanted to strike out on his own back then and leave his father's drunken rages behind, he hadn't been able to abandon his youngest brother to fend for himself.

Nor could he send this six-year-old girl into the mountain wilderness to face whatever might befall her and her mother.

Swallowing down the knot that clogged his throat, he met Caleb's gaze and nodded. "I'll make sure they get to their village."

Despite the fact that he already regretted the words, he would do whatever it took to see the woman and child to safety.

And then, he'd walk away.

CHAPTER 2

"Shhh." Watkuese pressed a finger to her lips and released a tiny hiss to catch her daughter's attention in the darkness.

Pop-pank didn't seem to hear her warning, just continued scraping leather against buckskin as she pulled the straps of her pack over her shoulders. The sound seemed to echo in the midnight air.

Light snoring still drifted from inside the lodge they'd shared with Otskai and her family. If any of them awoke, they would try to stop Watkuese from leaving under cover of darkness.

She wanted no more delays. Her spirit pressed to be gone. To be free of this place.

Not that she wasn't happy for the time spent with Otskai and this group of friends who had become like family to her cousin. Much of the visit had been enjoyable as they'd welcomed her and Pop-pank into their group. But this weight inside her, this pressing of her spirit...if she didn't leave now, she might not be able to stand one more day.

With Pop-pank's pack adjusted, Watkuese repositioned her own, then straightened. They were ready.

She reached out for her daughter's hand, but the girl pulled away.

A pain pressed Watkuese's chest, a combination of frustration and worry. Pop-pank hadn't been like this before. Not this sullen child who seemed determined to make things harder for Watkuese. Was it the loss of her parents that caused the change? Or had Watkuese already failed her charge?

She ignored the defiant action and waved her daughter forward as she took her own first step toward the edge of camp. And freedom.

Pop-pank fell into step behind her. As they set out across the grassland toward the first of the mountain ranges they would need to cross, Watkuese kept the girl in sight at the edge of her vision—just in case Pop-pank tried one of her disappearing games in the dark.

Watkuese didn't speak until they reached the cover of the trees climbing the base of the first hill, lest their voices carry back to the village behind them. When they had stepped into the pines and aspen, she turned to her daughter. "Does your pack fit well?"

"It's too heavy." Pop-pank's voice took on that nasal tone that grated on Watkuese's patience.

"I only put a few things inside." In truth, Watkuese could have carried everything on her own back, but she wanted her daughter to understand that hard work was part of life. The pack was mostly a symbol.

"I don't know why we have to walk. Naplág gave us horses to ride. We should be taking the horses."

Watkuese brushed the whining tone aside, but she'd heard this argument enough. She would give the explanation once more. "Those horses belong to your grandfather. Our home is too far away to take them. Aunt Otskai will see they get back to him."

Watkuese's father had intended to give them the horses, but she couldn't stand the thought of taking a valuable gift like that from his hand. She had nothing to give him in trade for them, and she'd promised herself when she first left her father's village that she would make her own way.

"Let's keep moving." Watkuese glanced back to make sure Pop-pank stayed close.

Thankfully, her daughter followed without another complaint. The trees shielded them from much of the light of the half moon, making it harder for Watkuese to pick out a safe path up the hill. As steep as this incline felt, the true mountains would be much more challenging to maneuver.

Just when Watkuese had settled into a steady stride, another whine sounded from behind.

"I'm tired. I need to stop."

She worked for a smile, then turned and reached out for her daughter. "Hold my hand, and I'll help pull you up the hill."

The girl shook her head, but her defiant look stretched into a yawn.

Watkuese's heart squeezed. Perhaps this wasn't fair, asking her daughter to travel during the dark of night. She'd thought it would feel like a great adventure to the girl. Watkuese certainly would have seen it as such when she was six.

But Pop-pank seemed so different from the outgoing, determined child Watkuese had been. Even different from the sweet, affectionate girl Pop-pank had been when Watkuese first met her. Would she return to that loveable child once the grieving time had passed?

Watkuese closed the distance to take the girl's hand, and Pop-pank didn't pull away this time. "Come along, my love. We'll manage the journey together. And we'll be thankful once we arrive home again."

Hand-in-hand, Watkuese half-pulling the child, they finally reached the summit and began the descent on the other side. At the top, Pop-pank had yanked free of Watkuese's hand, but on the easier downhill slope, the girl should be able to manage without help.

The leaf-covered ground grew slippery in areas, especially when layers of ice crunched beneath her feet. She'd almost waited too long to cross the mountains before winter turned the peaks even more treacherous. At least the first snowfall hadn't come yet.

Her foot slid beneath her, and she scrambled to catch her balance, gripping a sapling to stay upright. She glanced back to make sure Pop-pank didn't slip in the same place.

No movement flashed in the darkness behind her. Watkuese turned and peered up the hill. Had the girl fallen farther back? "Pop-pank!"

She held her breath as she listened for the reply. The icy hand of dread pressed on her chest. Surely Pop-pank wouldn't play her hiding game now. Not in the dark and cold. Not when they were both weary and trying to cover as much distance as they could before daylight.

She started back up the slope, peering around every tree she passed. "Pop-pank, please come out. This isn't the time to hide." The cold no longer pinched as anxiety sparked heat inside her.

What if she didn't come out on her own this time? By herself in the darkness, Watkuese might take hours to find her. And if Pop-pank took it into her mind to return to the Nez Perce village, how would Watkuese know? Surely she wouldn't run away. She was only playing a simple game of hiding, like before.

Watkuese paused, drawing in a deep breath to steady herself. "Pop-pank. Come to me now." She kept her voice firm yet did her best not to let frustration seep into her tone. If Pop-pank thought she would be punished, she might not be as likely to reveal herself.

As she scanned every tree and shadow around her, Watkuese strained to hear the snap of a twig, the crunch of a leaf, or a tiny sigh of breath.

Nothing.

The worry inside her tightened into fear. How could the girl stay so quiet? Maybe she really had run, yet how could she have sprinted so far—without a sound?

She took in another deep breath and raised her voice to carry farther. "Pop-pank! Come now."

After listening for a few disappointing heartbeats, she started up the hill again. She couldn't stand still and wait. When she finally did discover the girl, she wouldn't allow her out of her sight again. Not for any reason.

As she neared the top of the slope, the crunch of footsteps in leaves on the other side of the peak made her slow. The sound carried was louder than a young girl's tromping. The noise built in the quiet night. It must be animals, but not the tender steps of a deer or antelope. The stride wasn't right for a bear. Perhaps horses?

She sidled over to the nearest large tree, turning her body so the trunk hid most of her. Horses usually meant men. And any men out riding in the middle of the night weren't likely to have good intentions.

Pop-pank.

Panic clutched her throat. Had the approaching strangers found her daughter? How could she have let the girl out of her sight, even for a moment? The child was only six summers old. Though she'd become strong-willed, she had no understanding of the danger these hills and woods possessed.

Hats rose above the crest of the hill, then faces, though the darkness cloaked them in too many shadows for her to tell if she'd seen these men before or not. The second figure rode a little behind the first, and she waited to see if any more outlines would appear.

Only the two.

She slid her gaze over the pair again as they descended the hill. The men's clothing proclaimed them to be white, and something about their silhouettes seemed familiar. But then her gaze landed on the unusual blaze on the first horse's face. A sideways star that spread over one eye, and below that a smaller snip of white just above the nose. No other horse could have that exact marking.

She slid her focus upward again. Yes, those broad shoulders belonged to him.

Hugh Charpentier. The other fellow riding just behind—she could see his frame better now—had Louis's leaner build.

She eased out a breath, though the tension didn't leave her shoulders. Why were these men out here in the middle of the night? If someone from the village had come after her, wouldn't it be Otskai or her husband Caleb? She'd spoken to these two so rarely, they could only be called acquaintances.

Had they, too, sneaked away from camp?

A new worry needled in. They had no reason to leave in the dead of night unless they were running. Perhaps they'd stolen something?

A flash of anger seared through her. If they'd taken something that belonged to her people, she wouldn't allow them to escape unhindered.

Withdrawing her knife from the sheath hanging at her neck, she raised it to a throwing position. She didn't give herself time to think about what she was doing, just stepped out from behind the tree. "Halt!"

Hugh responded within the same breath, jerking his reins tight to stop his horse even as his other hand moved to the rifle laying across his lap.

"Don't touch your weapons." She barked the words loud enough to fill the space between them. She'd heard the men speak in the Shoshone tongue—or rather the Snake tongue, as the white men call that people. Neither Hugh nor Louis spoke the language fluently, but they seemed to know enough to communicate. That would give her the upper hand in the conversation.

Louis had reined in his horse beside his brother's, and both men slowly raised their hands away from their guns.

"What are you doing here in the middle of the night?" She kept her blade pointed toward Hugh. He would definitely be the stronger threat of the two. Louis's personality was so easy-going, it seemed impossible to think he would do something to harm her.

But men weren't always the way they appeared.

"Looking for you." Hugh glanced around. "And your daughter. Where is she?"

A likely story. Watkuese fought the urge to scan the area herself. She had to keep looking for Pop-pank. But first, she had to get rid of these men. "Why would you be looking for me?"

"Your cousin and her husband sent us. Caleb told me last night he thought you'd take off soon. It was a stroke of luck I saw you and the girl leave in the darkness. I woke Caleb and your cousin to let them know we were headed out to catch up with you."

She hesitated. Could his words be true? Had Otskai really expected her to leave? Her cousin knew her better than anyone else, so she might well have seen Watkuese's unrest. But why wouldn't Otskai have talked to her instead of commissioning these near strangers to follow her?

Maybe a few more questions would help her know if he spoke the truth or not. "How did my cousin react when you told her I'd left?"

She couldn't see the nuance of his expression across the distance with shadows darkening his face, but she did make out a frown. "She seemed sad. Said she'd hoped for a chance to say goodbye to you and your daughter."

He glanced around once more. "Where is the girl anyway? Have you made camp here?"

The urgency to forget about this questioning and find the young life entrusted to her tightened every part of Watkuese's body. One more inquiry, then she'd send these men on their way and find her daughter. "Why would Otskai ask you? Why not send Caleb to bring us back?" She could understand why her cousin wouldn't wish to venture out into the cold night herself, what with the new baby growing inside her that made Otskai so sick. But surely Caleb would have come.

Not that Watkuese would have returned with him. At least she could have sent back a farewell to her cousin.

He remained quiet a moment, maybe searching for words in the Shoshone language. "We did not come to bring you back. Caleb asked us to ride with you. To see you safely to your village." Once more he peered around, this time nudging his horse forward to close the distance between them. "Where is Pop-pank? She's safe, isn't she? Not hiding again?"

Now that he'd drawn near, the piercing stare he leveled at her showed all too clearly in the partial moonlight. A jolt of anger shot through her. "I would have already found her if you two hadn't come. We've no need for you to travel with us. You can go on about your business."

He was already spinning his horse and straining to see into the darkness. "Where did you see her last? Have you found her tracks?"

As much as frustration made her want to shake the man, the thought of having two others help her hunt slid a thin layer of worry from her shoulders.

Still, she paused another moment before responding. Did she dare trust them? Otskai had seemed to. And the others in their group. These two men had lived among the villagers for several moons now. She could at least allow them to help find Pop-pank.

CHAPTER 3

*W*atkuese motioned down the hill she'd just traipsed back up. "We were walking that way. I slipped on an icy spot, and when I looked back to speak to Pop-pank, she was gone."

Hugh slid from his horse, and Louis did the same. With long strides, the older brother started down the way she'd pointed. "Show me where. Maybe we can find her tracks."

Though she hated retracing her steps once more instead of searching new ground, the confident way Hugh stepped in to help eased a bit of her panic. As she walked, she cupped her hands around her mouth and raised her voice again. "Pop-pank! Come to me. Come now, D—." She barely stopped herself from calling the girl *daughter*.

Pop-pank *was* her daughter as far as she was concerned. She'd promised the child's parents she would love and raise her as her own. But though eight moons had come and gone since their passing, Watkuese still heard Pop-pank's tears some nights. She always drew her close, cradling her and speaking soothing words until the crying eased.

She'd noticed in those grief-filled moments that any time

Watkuese spoke the word *daughter*, Pop-Pank's body seemed to coil tight. It wasn't that Watkuese wanted to take Kimana's place as her mother. No one could ever replace such a sweet, loving, giving soul—especially not Watkuese. But she wanted Pop-pank to know she was loved. She would never be on her own, stranded without family. The two of them had each other and always would.

But not if Watkuese lost the girl.

"Pop-pank!" She screamed the name into the darkness, desperation renewing inside her.

Still no answer. The only sounds were the crackling of the horses' hooves in front of her.

"Is this the ice you slipped on?"

Hugh's voice drew her focus, and she studied the plants around him. "Yes."

He handed his reins to his brother and crouched low to the ground. After a few heartbeats, he half-stood and moved back up the hill, still peering hard at the winter brown grass. If only a bit of snow covered the ground so the tracks would be clear. She'd never been good at reading signs, but maybe this man possessed the skills to show them which way her daughter had gone.

Hugh moved slowly for several steps, then he paused, his focus shifting to the left.

Hope clutched in her chest. When he turned to walk that direction, she started after him. "Is this the way she went?"

He didn't answer, and she strained to see what he might have spotted. The darkness cast shadows through the grass and trees. How could he decipher anything? He kept padding forward, bent over to study the ground as he moved.

She could assume the answer to her question was *yes*. After all, he wouldn't pursue this path if the tracks didn't look promising. But it raised her ire that he'd ignored her. She hated being at the mercy of others, especially a man she barely knew.

A glance back at the younger brother, who led the horses behind them, showed the moonlight slanted at just the right angle to see his features—and the concerned expression on his face.

Louis caught her gaze. "We'll find her. Hugh is the best tracker I know. He can spot anything." His voice possessed a soothing certainty that eased her frustration with the elder brother. Just because the man rarely found a civil tongue didn't mean he wasn't an excellent tracker. If he could find Pop-pank, she wouldn't care if he ever spoke to her again.

As much as Watkuese chafed at strolling along behind this man while her daughter waited somewhere out in the darkness —perhaps in danger—if he really had found Pop-pank's trail, staying with him was wise.

"I remember back when we were young, still living with this family named Heinrich." Louis's voice sounded from behind her again, loud enough to be heard but soft enough not to distract his brother's focus. "I was just a little thing, but Hugh was older, of course. They would always send him out to bring in the milk cows in the evening because he was the only one who could tell which tracks were fresh. He'd find those animals in half the time either of the two Heinrich girls could manage."

A grunt sounded from the man ahead of her. "They could have accomplished it faster if they wanted to. Even a tot could track cows."

"You've a gift, brother. I could name at least thirty other times you've proven to be a superior tracker. If anyone can find little Poppy, it's you."

If fear didn't clutch so tight around her throat, Watkuese might have smiled at the odd version of Pop-pank's name. But a strong part of her wanted to shush the man so Hugh could focus on his *superior tracking*.

The older brother paused mid-stride, and she sidestepped so

she didn't run into him. He turned around and waved for Louis to back the horses. Had he lost the tracks?

After a moment of scanning the ground, his focus lifted to a pair of trees—a thick sapling hugged up against a larger trunk. The many branches of the sapling would allow a child to maneuver up them, and the older tree would provide sturdiness to support her weight.

Hope rose in Watkuese as she peered up into the limbs, but darkness didn't allow her to see far. "Pop-pank?" If the girl was up there, she was trying to stay hidden. But why? Did she really not want to return to their home?

Perhaps she simply couldn't stand any more time in Watkuese's company. Pain burned her throat as that thought settled. How could she fix this? How could she make Pop-pank understand she only wanted to help?

"Poppy, want to come down and ride my horse?" Louis's voice held his usual lighthearted ring.

When a branch rustled in response, Watkuese's breath stilled. Would Pop-pank actually come down for the offer? She seemed to love playing with Louis, especially when he teased or bent down on her level to play games the children loved.

"Is that Snowy?" The small voice sounded in the darkness directly above.

"Sure is. He came all this way to take you for a ride."

The child knew the horse's name? The branch rustled again, and moccasined feet appeared through the darkness. Then Pop-pank's leggings and tunic became clear as she descended.

Watkuese stepped forward to help guide the child's steps and catch her if her feet slipped.

When Pop-pank reached the bottom branch, she turned and held out a hand to Louis. "Lift me onto her."

Louis glanced at Watkuese, seeking permission. It was a bit late to ask now, but Watkuese nodded. Containing the girl on the horse would be good. And how could she say no when her daughter finally sounded eager?

As Louis hoisted the girl off the branch and onto the saddle, Watkuese's chest burned. Her daughter hadn't even acknowledged her presence, but at least she was safe. If only the girl would *want* to turn to Watkuese for comfort.

While they traipsed single file back toward the trail she'd been following down the hill, she re-centered her thoughts on what should happen next. She and Pop-pank needed time alone to find their own way. Somehow, she had to make these men leave.

And in the process, she had to keep Pop-pank from sneaking back with them.

~

*I*t felt as though grit clogged Hugh's eyes, but he squinted in the early dawn light to focus on the meat sizzling in the pan. He'd had just enough smoked bear meat left to feed all of them this morning and pack a meal to eat on the trail.

He'd need to hunt as they rode today. Watkuese probably carried food, but he didn't intend to eat her fare unless he could find nothing else. If he and Louis were trapping, they'd have all the meat they needed. But not when traveling on a journey like this.

A flash of movement caught his eye, and he forced himself to look up slowly, his movements measured. He'd been waiting for this, and he wanted her to know he'd been watching.

Watkuese froze under his gaze, her eyes locking with his. She didn't wear the look of one caught sneaking. Instead, she lifted her chin, and her gaze attempted to flash fire at him, though the look lost some of its force from the remnants of sleep that softened her features.

"Going somewhere?" He dropped his focus from her eyes to the pack slung across her back, then down her arm to where she clutched Pop-pank's hand. The child looked half-asleep, leaning into Watkuese's hold as if to keep herself upright.

"We're leaving." If anything, the woman's jaw locked in an even more defiant look.

He nodded toward the meat. "The food is ready. Full bellies will give us all strength for the day's travel." He glanced toward Pop-pank and tried for a smile. "Growing girls especially need a hearty breakfast."

Pop-pank's mouth curved in a shy grin.

Hugh turned his focus back to the pan. The meat was beginning to smoke, so he pulled the cookware away from the flame. Perhaps he'd let it sizzle a bit too long.

Across the fire, Louis's blankets shifted. His brother didn't usually climb from his covers until he had to, but Hugh had been trying to adjust that habit for months now. Maybe Louis would finally become an early riser on this journey.

Hugh shifted his focus back to Watkuese, then motioned to a clear spot of ground beside the fire. "Sit. Eat. We'll head out as soon as we finish."

The reluctance on her face was hard to miss, but she led the girl forward and dropped her pack, then they both lowered to the ground.

He would have doled out food for each of them, but he had no idea how much a woman and child ate in the morning, so he pushed the pan in in front of Watkuese and set the two plates beside it. She probably used bark plates normally, but he had none, only the tinware he and Louis carried.

No one spoke as they all ate. Watkuese eyed him warily, probably frustrated he'd stalled her escape. Pop-pank and Louis both wore dazed, half-asleep expressions. Though Louis could talk well enough later in the day, he wasn't usually good for conversation until the sun had dried the dew from the grass.

As for himself, Hugh spent the meal doing his best to remember landmarks they should watch out for today. He'd taken this route on a few hunting trips but didn't remember much past the first few hills. As long as he kept them headed east, though, they wouldn't be lost.

After the meal, they packed up, and he expected Watkuese to argue once more against him and Louis accompanying her. But she didn't. While he and his brother settled their horses and strapped their gear behind, she doused the remaining coals and set their camp to rights.

He pulled his cinch strap tight, then gave his gelding a pat and turned to Watkuese. "There's room on Louis's saddle for the girl to ride with him. You can take my horse."

Her brows rose, then she glanced at his gelding. "Where will you ride?" Her tone sounded measured, as though waiting for him to say the wrong thing.

If she thought he'd force her to ride with him, he could set her right on that score. It rankled that she'd jump to such an unkind conclusion. "I'll be walking." Not his preferred transportation across the mountains, but it would toughen him up some.

The relief he'd expected on her face didn't come. Instead, she shook her head. Hard. And her gaze narrowed on him. "*You* ride your horse. I was planning to walk."

There would be a flood in the desert before he rode a horse while a woman walked beside him, especially up and down the mountains.

But before he could state that fact, Louis stepped up beside him. "Come on, Poppy. Snowy's ready for you."

The girl scampered to his younger brother and wrapped her arms around the gray gelding's neck. That was the way a female should respond to a chivalrous offer.

After Louis hoisted the child into the saddle, Hugh turned his focus back to the mother. Watkuese no longer stood by the remnant of campfire ashes. She'd moved in front of the horses, positioned to start out ahead of them. Clearly not planning to mount his horse.

Hugh grasped for his most diplomatic tone. "Please. I'd like you to ride my horse today. He's a sturdy mount, surefooted in the mountains." Just as capable on a cliffside as the mule Hugh had traded for him, and much faster.

Watkuese spared him a glance. "I wish to walk." Then she turned toward the trail and started out.

The soft chuckle from Louis's direction only raised Hugh's frustration. He couldn't very well hoist her into the saddle, so it looked like they'd both be walking. A waste of a good horse.

The last thing he wanted was to see the humor sparking in his brother's eyes, so Hugh kept his focus forward as he led his gelding onto the path behind the most stubborn woman he'd ever met.

CHAPTER 4

*E*xhaustion pulled at Watkuese, but she forced her shoulders not to bend under the weight of weariness as she climbed the mountainside. If only she walked *behind* the horses so both men wouldn't be watching her every move— likely waiting for her to show weakness. But she'd set out that morning in the lead, and falling behind might make them think she couldn't bear the journey. Besides, she wasn't certain either of them knew the route to her village.

At least Pop-pank was able to ride instead of walking. The lilting tone of her daughter's voice drifted forward, though Watkuese couldn't understand the words from this distance. Louis's chuckle made her wish even more she knew what she'd said.

Pop-pank seemed to be enjoying herself. Louis had a way with her that brought back the sweet girlish temperament she'd had before her parents died. The thought twisted a painful longing in Watkuese's chest. Maybe Pop-pank's pleasure would be worth allowing these two men to accompany them.

As the incline steepened and became littered with fist-sized stones, Watkuese's breath came in deeper gulps. As the hours had passed, her legs had lost much of their strength, but she didn't dare ask for a rest. The sun had only moved a finger width across the sky since they'd stopped for the midday meal.

She adjusted her path up the slope so they weren't climbing so steeply. They might need to track back and forth up the incline to reach the top, but that would be better for the horses too.

Bringing up the rear, Hugh still led his gelding instead of riding. The man must possess more stubbornness than good sense if he was willing to waste a perfectly good mount. Was he as exhausted as she?

Perhaps if she called a stop, he would be grateful. After all—

Her foot caught on the edge of a rock, throwing her sideways. She scrambled to right herself, but her balance shifted downhill, and her ankle bent at a sharp angle. She landed on her knee first, then her hands struck the stony ground. She pressed hard to keep from rolling as the pack tried to propel her down the slope.

At last, she stilled in that awkward position. Her body began to tremble as the pain set in. First her knee, then the burn on her palms. But the fire in her ankle soon rose above the rest.

"Are you hurt?" Hugh's deep voice sounded above her just before the weight of the pack lifted off her back. He eased the bundle over her head, but she would have to lift one hand for him to remove it completely.

Biting her lip to keep from crying out with the pain, she lifted that arm and allowed him to pull the pack away.

He crouched beside her, bringing his face level with hers. "Where are you hurt?"

Her hands and knee were likely only scraped, though they burned as though she knelt in leaping flames. But her ankle...

She eased sideways to sit and had to blink to keep back tears as a hundred knives speared her ankle. What had she done? How could she travel through the mountains with an injury?

Hugh spotted the source of her pain and wrapped both his hands around her foot to help position it better. She should rebuke him for touching her, but his help lessened the agony—a little, at least. Besides, if she spoke, her voice would crack under the weight of the tears building inside her.

He pulled his hand away from her moccasin but studied the place. "Can you move your foot?"

She was fairly certain she'd not broken a bone, and though the effort sent a new shot of fire up her leg, she did manage to lift her toes upward.

"Glad nothing's broken. But the ankle is already swelling." He turned to search around them. "You should soak it in cold water—if we can find a creek." His focus honed on the crest of the mountain above them. "I think there might be a stream running through the next valley."

His gaze found her face. "Better to leave your moccasin on to keep the swelling down until we get there. Where else are you hurt? Your hands? Your knees?"

With the pain squeezing out her breath, she didn't have the strength to speak. She allowed him to reach for her wrists and turn them so he could see her palms.

A wince twisted his expression. "We'll clean them up when we get to water. Is your knee worse than this?"

She shook her head.

"I'm going to lift you onto my horse. Can you ride by yourself?" Somewhere in the midst of his questions, his voice had grown gentle. Maybe that was why the last one didn't rankle as it might have.

She nodded. There was no way she could walk up the mountain and down the other side, but perhaps she could make it to his horse. How awful this would be if she were alone with Poppank—if these two brothers hadn't come along to help. But she couldn't let her thoughts follow that trail.

When he moved beside her and held out his arms as though

he planned to pick her up, she motioned him back. She could do this. She *would*.

But as she turned onto her hands and knees again, the fire in her ankle raged so fiercely that it took her breath away. Hands under her arms lifted her, and all she could do was hold her breath to keep from crying out.

He stood her up on her good foot for a moment as he adjusted his hold, then he lifted her onto the saddle. She sat sideways at first, gathering strength to lift her leg up and over the horse's neck. But Hugh was already taking action. He cradled one hand under her foot and the other beneath her leg as he lifted. She took over his hold as she lowered the limb to sit the saddle properly.

At last, the man stood beside the horse, staring up at her. His perceptive gaze sought too much. She was too weak to hide her pain.

But he didn't press his advantage. Just gathered up the reins and said, "Hold on."

$\sim$

*A*s Hugh halted his gelding at the edge of the stream, his gaze lifted to the darkening sky. Rain would come soon, and he needed to find shelter. If it were just him and Louis, they would keep going under the protection of their hats. But a woman and child needed cover. Especially with the cold wind blowing through this valley and Watkuese injured.

First, he had to settle her so she could soak her foot. Turning to the woman, he took in the slump of her shoulders as she clutched the saddle. Her pain must be awful. Even as exhausted as she'd been hiking up the mountain, she'd not let the sharp line of her shoulders bow. Nothing like they did now.

She started to dismount on her own, so he strode quickly around to the gelding's other side. He scooped her into his arms, and just like before, his body sprang to life at the feel of her. Had he ever held a woman this close? He'd always kept himself far away from females, and for good reason. She felt too good tucked against him, every part of him too aware. One touch made him long for another. Made it hard to let her go.

But he forced himself to lower her at the bank's edge. She reached for her moccasin lacing, and he allowed her to handle the task of removing them.

Better he back away.

He nearly stepped on Pop-pank as the girl scooted around him to drop beside her mother. She seemed in much better spirits than she'd been the night before, the tension between mother and daughter gone.

Good. He'd hated the pained look on Watkuese's face as the child stayed with Louis and ignored her.

He couldn't imagine having a mother like Watkuese and not adoring her. His own ma had been very different from this Indian woman in both looks and mannerisms, but he could still remember the love that shimmered in her eyes when she looked at him—the same love that glowed when Watkuese watched her daughter. How could the girl not be drawn to that?

He didn't know their story, but he had a feeling something was unique about these two. There was always more than one could see from the outside. As much as he tried to keep himself distant from all people, a part of him craved insight about this little family.

He turned back to his horse. His time would be better spent finding shelter before icy rain pelted them all.

After searching at least a quarter hour, the best shelter he could find was a cluster of trees beside a rock overhang. They could stretch furs over the branches to give them enough protected space. This might only be a short downpour, though the thickness of the clouds made it look like the rain would continue a while.

Watkuese needed time to rest that leg. Several days would be best, but he had a feeling she wouldn't sit still that long.

Maybe he could keep her here for at least one day.

When he returned to the others, Louis had the females fascinated with a story about the two dogs who'd lived at the livery where he last worked.

Watkuese looked up and met his gaze as he approached. Her dark eyes were so beautiful, one of the features that always snagged his attention. When she fixed them on him as she did in that moment, they drew him in.

He dismounted. "I found a place that should give some shelter." Moving to Watkuese's side, he crouched and studied her foot, still soaking in the water. "Feeling any better?"

She pulled the leg from the stream. "I can walk now."

He certainly wouldn't allow her to walk, not considering how swollen the ankle had been only an hour before. Not while he still had the strength to carry her. "Better let the ankle rest. I don't mind lifting you into the saddle."

In fact, as near as he was right now, his body hummed with the desire to take her in his arms again. He tried to keep his manner relaxed as he tucked one arm under her knees and the other around her back. She was so willowy, it didn't surprise him that lifting her wasn't a burden.

Before, she'd remained stiff in his arms, but this time her head tucked against his shoulder and she seemed to relax into him. Perhaps the pain had finally exhausted her, but somehow this felt more like trust then weariness.

He almost hated to set her on the horse, for he'd have to let go and pull away. But Louis had already hoisted Pop-pank in the saddle behind him, and the air had grown thick with moisture. Any moment, the first drops would fall, and he wanted to have Watkuese and Pop-pank tucked safely beneath the shelter.

Once he placed Watkuese in the saddle, she gripped the leather and turned a tight smile to him. It was getting harder and harder to see her in pain. Was there not something more he could do to bring relief? He could think of nothing, save getting her to a resting place. Perhaps he could carry water for her to soak the ankle again once they made camp.

With him leading the gelding and Louis's mount following, they trekked up the valley to the cover he'd found. The first few raindrops fell when they'd only ridden halfway. By the time they reached the rock overhang, water soaked them all.

He had no time to enjoy tucking Watkuese against him this time. He swept her off the horse and settled her under the ledge. Pop-pank scampered in beside her, and Watkuese snuggled her daughter close, as a mother hen would. The rain pelted like ice, but the stone protected them from the water and most of the wind.

He and Louis worked quickly to unroll their furs and tie them up to create a space large enough to build a fire. As night fell, they would need the warmth and dry clothes its heat would offer.

At last, they had the horses settled and their gear tucked under the shelter. Watkuese had nurtured a small flame using the dry wood they carried with them for a situation just like this. Enough dead branches littered the ground under the trees that they were able to find and bring in the rest of what they'd need for the night so the wood could begin drying around the fire's circle. Hugh paused to sweep the camp with his glance. What else should be done?

Water for Watkuese's ankle.

As he turned toward the pack to find the pot, Louis gripped his shoulder. "Everything else can wait. Let's rest until the rain stops."

Hugh shook his head and pulled out of his brother's grasp. "Just one more..."

But Louis stepped into his path, forcing him to halt. Then he pointed under the overhang. "Sit."

Rarely did Louis insist on anything, especially not with that tone. Maybe the rain would end soon and Hugh could retrieve fresh water then. At least, he could wait for a while to see.

Once Hugh nodded, Louis plopped himself beside Pop-pank and ruffled her hair before stretching out his legs and settling against the rock behind them. That meant the only dry place left to sit was at Watkuese's side. He ignored the leap in his chest and schooled his expression as he sank in the spot.

As Louis had, he eased back against the stone and extended his legs in front of him. Only a handbreadth of space separated him and the woman, and he did his best to ignore her nearness. And fight the urge to look at her.

The rain drowned out the crackle of the fire as they waited, none of them speaking. At least a quarter hour passed, then another, and maybe a full hour. Hugh added logs to the fire to keep a hearty blaze, though they'd all dried by now. Pop-pank fell asleep against her mother's arm, and Watkuese lowered the girl's head to her lap. As she stroked the thick, glossy hair in a steady rhythm, the movement drew his gaze to her long fingers. He could almost imagine what that gentle stroking must feel like, and his throat went dry at the thought.

What was wrong with him? How had he lost his good sense? His fingers crept up to the curved scar on his temple. That blow three years before had been enough to bring him around the one time he truly *had* lost his senses. It had shown him how much he was like his father. How strong drink could control him and turn him into the man he hated above all others.

That reminder bolstered him now, and he straightened, adding a bit more space between him and the beauty beside him. He would never put a woman through what his mother had endured. As much as he hated to admit it, he really did have too much of his father in him.

Better he brace himself and put more distance between him and his thoughts about Watkuese.

Springing to his feet, he reached for the pot. Then he charged out into the rain, welcoming the icy pelts.

As his body grew numb from wet and cold, his mind finally came clear. For her protection, he had to stay far away from Watkuese. He'd get her safely to her village, then he and Louis would be on their own—as he should be.

CHAPTER 5

*W*atkuese struggled through the fog in her mind as she blinked in the dim light. Why had she wanted to rise so early?

Awareness settled around her, along with the warmth of the small body curled beside her. The rain had finally stopped sometime in the night. And now that morning had come, she needed to rekindle the fire and prepare a meal.

As she worked to sit up, fire shot through her ankle, clouding her mind once again. Was it really so important she be the first one up and cooking?

Yes.

Perhaps if she told herself that a few more times, her body would agree. After Hugh's comments the morning before about a growing girl needing food, she'd determined to be the one to awaken early and have food sizzling over the fire. Though she'd not always prepared a formal meal, she'd always made sure Poppank had plenty to eat, even when times were lean. As long as they traveled together, though, she would give that man no cause to question her mothering ability.

Despite the pain, she had warm salmon and camas cakes

ready when Hugh sat up from his covers. She'd not packed enough to feed all of them for the entire journey, but surely he'd brought food they could share later. For now, the sleepy pleasure on his face as he looked at the meal slid warmth through her.

She couldn't bring herself to meet his gaze, though. There was something too intimate about being the only ones awake in the early morning light. She reached for one of his tin plates. "Are you hungry?"

"I am. I'll get a load of firewood first though." He stood in a smooth motion that bespoke the lithe muscle hidden beneath his trapper's clothing. When he turned and padded quietly out of camp and into the grove of trees beyond, she allowed herself to watch for only a few heartbeats. She couldn't deny how the man gave pleasure to the eyes. But it was the rest of him—and how she felt about that rest of him—that she still couldn't decide about.

He returned, looking more awake and burdened with both arms full of wood. The logs clattered to the ground near enough to the fire that the flame would dry them, and the sounds made Louis stir beneath his blanket.

Soon enough, they all sat around the low flames eating the food she'd warmed. The question that had been nudging at her all morning had to be broached. She hated requesting favors, but she could see no way around this one. Hugh probably wouldn't object, not when he'd all but insisted yesterday, but asking for help...

At last, she swallowed down the dry knot in her throat and addressed the man. "Will you be riding your horse today?"

He paused partway through chewing a bite of camas cake and studied her. His throat worked as he swallowed the food, then his voice came out casually. "No."

Relief eased through her, giving her boldness for the next question. "May I ride him then?"

He was still watching her, and he paused for a single heart-beat before answering. "No."

Disbelief flared in her chest for a quick moment, then heat simmered through her. He would really withhold a mount from an injured woman when he didn't plan to ride that animal himself? Just when she'd begun to think kind thoughts about him...

But he spoke again before she could set loose her ire. "I don't think we should travel today. As cold as it is, some of that rain and mud will turn to ice. Your leg could use a day to rest. And that will give me a chance to do some hunting. I'd like to stock up enough meat for the rest of the journey."

She didn't miss the way he hid her weakness between two other reasons to wait. Still, she had a feeling her ankle was the main reason he wanted to keep them here. More food would be helpful though—necessary even. If they rode today, she would endure it without complaint. But if hunting gave them a valid reason to wait...perhaps she should acquiesce.

Still, she had to slip in a final comment. "I don't need to rest."

He raised his brows and shrugged. "I *do* need to hunt." The finality in his tone eased away any need for her to press the matter further.

"Tell you what." Louis's voice still graveled with the remnants of sleep. "Hugh can go hunting, and Poppy and I will do a bit of exploring." He sent the girl a wink, once more smoothing out the tension.

If only the peace could last.

~

*B*y the time the sun nearly reached its zenith, Hugh had only brought down a small deer and a fox. Enough to last a few days if they rationed, but probably not the entire trip. He needed to return to camp and check on the others, though.

He'd been relieved when Watkuese finally laid down to rest. And with Louis keeping Pop-pank occupied, Hugh had hoped to bring in enough food to carry them a fortnight. If the weather stayed warm enough, they should reach the other side of the mountains in less than a week, but he'd rather have more food than strictly necessary, just in case. You never knew when that first snowfall would come, especially in the heights of the Rockies.

*W*hen he returned, their camp was deserted except for their belongings. Only a few small flames leaping from the coals showed someone had been there recently.

He scanned the area. Watkuese might be napping, and he certainly didn't want to wake her. But except for two furs laid out to sit on, the rest of the bedding had been rolled and stacked neatly. "Watkuese?"

The fire snapped, and a gust of wind whipped up, chilling his nose and cheeks. Perhaps that was the reason the fine hairs on his neck rose on end.

"Watkuese?" He stepped around the fire, checked once more over the area where they'd all slept the night before, then glanced at the landscape beyond the circle of their camp. Pockets of trees littered most of the view, but he could see no people among them. Maybe behind the boulder that stretched across one side of their camp.

He started around the massive stone, and when he reached the backside and found nobody, he raised his voice to call up the rock-strewn slope. "Watkuese! Louis, Pop-pank!" The wind whipped his voice back against him, but no one was climbing up or down the hill. Where in thunder had they all gone?

That tingle on his neck had turned into worry shooting through him. He finished circling the rock, then marched through camp once more. Maybe they'd gone to water the horses, though Watkuese shouldn't have strayed so far from camp. Had she taken leave of her senses to walk on that ankle? This was supposed to be a day of rest, but the break would be wasted if she overtaxed the injury.

The hike to water took several minutes, definitely too far for Watkuese to have hobbled. As he neared, the murmur of voices reached him even before he saw his companions.

Pop-pank's high tone came first, then Louis's low tenor. At last, the rich melody of Watkuese's voice answered them both. It's soothing tone did little to ease the anger building inside him. Not anger really—frustration. She needed to take better care of herself, not go wandering the countryside with her injury.

Louis's words were the first he could decipher. "...hope he comes back with a great big squash."

"What's a squash?" Pop-pank's curiosity rang clear.

"It's kind of like your camas root, except you don't have to dig for it. It grows from a vine and you pluck it off."

"Can you eat it like a berry?"

He was close enough to see Louis's nose scrunch into a sour face. "It's much better if you cook it."

Watkuese noticed Hugh's presence first, and she watched him with that intense gaze of hers as he closed the final distance between them.

The sight of her swept away the last of his anger, especially when his gaze dipped to her foot resting in a pool of water. "This is a bit far to have walked, don't you think?"

The straightening of her back was almost imperceptible, though it added a touch of the regal to her manner. Then her chin came up in that look of defiance he already knew well. "Your brother was kind enough to bring me on his horse."

Ah. He should have considered that. He should have brought her down on his own gelding.

Heat crept up his neck at his lapse, but he nodded. "Good." A glance toward her swollen limb showed that, though the water distorted the size, the swelling had gone down. "Soaking has helped?"

"I'll be ready to travel again tomorrow."

The cold water may have aided her injury, but it'd done nothing to lessen her stubbornness.

He shifted his focus to his brother, who sat with Pop-pank, both of them watching him with open curiosity. "I brought in a mule deer and a fox. You want to dress them and smoke the meat while I hunt in the other direction? Or do you want to hunt?" His brother might want some time to himself if he'd been keeping up with the child all morning.

Louis tipped his head as he studied Hugh. "I can handle the dirty work. You're better at finding the game trails."

Hugh raised his brows. "Maybe you'd better practice then." Hugh had made a living at trapping for more than a decade, but Louis wasn't incapable. The boy had done plenty of hunting— he'd had to keep food on the table when he lived alone with Pa. Was this an excuse to stay in camp, or did he think Hugh preferred to be out? Normally he would, but part of him didn't want to leave Watkuese. Just in case she needed help.

Not that she would ever admit a need.

But...better not to argue with his brother. He turned to Watkuese. "I can take you back to camp before I go."

Her gaze lifted to the sky above them. The trees in this area blocked the wind, but she sat in a small clearing that allowed the sun through. "I'd rather stay here a while longer." She sent a glance to Louis. "After that, I'll help clean and cook the meat and scrape the hides."

An unsettling suspicion needled as Hugh took in the three of them. Surely there wasn't some ill-fated attraction budding between these two. Louis was barely full grown. Though, at nineteen, he was three years older than Hugh had been when he'd set out on his own, but Louis still seemed too...young.

And Watkuese... Bile stung his belly at the thought. She was probably somewhere between Hugh's and Louis's ages, but she was...different. Definitely not right for his carefree brother.

Hugh's gaze slipped down to Pop-pank. Louis did seem to get along well with the girl, but that only meant he'd make a good nursemaid for an afternoon. It didn't have to count for anything more.

The child met Hugh's gaze. "I want to hunt too."

It took him a moment to make sense of the words, and not because she didn't speak clearly. They were so unexpected. Though she tucked her chin and narrowed her gaze at him in a manner very different from Watkuese's determined look, she used the same stubborn tone her mother did.

Hugh couldn't possibly take a child on a hunt, especially not a female. How old had Louis been when he'd first taken him hunting? It'd been after they were forced to return home, so the boy had been about six. Even then, Hugh had let the lad tag along only to keep him out of Pa's reach.

What if Pop-pank scared away the game? Worse, if he took her with him, that would make him responsible for her—the *only* one responsible for her. Not wise.

Shaking his head, he searched for a tone that would soften his answer. "That's not a good idea. You better stay and help your mother this time."

A flicker of hurt flashed through her eyes, but she turned her head away.

A matching pain pressed in his own chest. He'd had to say no. It was for her own good. But it had been so long since he'd been around children that he'd forgotten how much he hated disappointing them.

Crouching down, he brought himself closer to her level.

"Maybe Louis can take you on another exploring trip after he gets his work done."

She glanced back with the barest of nods, but if he weren't mistaken, that was still hurt in her expression. Surely doing anything with Louis would be more fun than sitting perched with him until her feet grew numb from cold.

He stood, avoiding all their gazes. "I'm headed back out then." Hunting by himself was exactly where he should be. When it came to other people, he never could get it right.

CHAPTER 6

*H*er ankle didn't throb.

Watkuese shifted her foot in the faint morning light. The movement shot fire up her leg. So much for the pain being gone, but at least she'd had that first moment without the constant ache.

Still, the injury must be healing, for the pulsing didn't pound throughout her entire body as it had yesterday. She would be able to ride today. No matter what, she would make sure they pushed on.

Hugh may have needed to hunt, but she knew coddling when she saw it. The last thing she wanted was for him to see her as weak. She'd been on her own for several years now, and she didn't need him to make decisions for her.

The quiet scuff of footsteps sounded, and she jerked her focus toward the muted darkness outside the light of the low campfire. Hugh emerged from the shadows, the sight of him easing the pounding in her chest.

But then disappointment pressed in. He carried a pot, water sloshing out as he dropped to his knees beside the fire. He'd been the first to rise and appeared to be already preparing the morning meal. Had she overslept? She should hobble over and insist that preparing the food for her daughter was her own task.

Or...she could lie there and watch him work. Some people might think seeing to women's tasks made a man appear weak, but watching Hugh Charpentier prepare a meal proved that opinion wrong in every way.

The breadth of his shoulders as he bent over his preparations, the half-sure half-clumsy way he scooped some kind of powder into the water, showed both his capability and a peek at the vulnerability most men tried to hide. And the strong lines of his face...

She'd never known a white man she considered handsome. Very few Nimiipuu or Shoshone men either, for that matter. Not once she knew their personality.

But Hugh... There was something different about him. She'd sensed it back in the Nimiipuu camp, but spending these past two days with him had made the truth plain. The quiet intensity—almost gruffness—that usually cloaked his actions sometimes peeled away to reveal a tenderness that stirred her spirit.

Like when he'd crouched down to speak to Pop-pank yesterday. Not only had he realized her daughter's disappointment, but he'd tried to make it better. If only his solution hadn't been to foist her on his brother and run.

With that reality settling in to shore up her defenses, Watkuese pulled one of her furs around her shoulders and sat up.

Hugh glanced her way, his expression hard to read. Maybe a hint of tenderness, but a wary look too.

She shifted her focus away from him and reached for a sapling she'd been using to help herself stand. Her aching body struggled to comply, but she finally made it to her feet.

Hugh moved toward her, a wooden pole in his hand. "I

found this last night. Thought it might help you keep the weight off that leg."

She examined the rod closer. About the thickness of her wrist and as tall as her shoulder, the bark had been pulled off and the surface rubbed smooth. It would be sturdy enough to help.

Help. The word always made her cringe. But refusing this would be foolish.

She lifted her gaze to his and nodded. "Thank you." Then she accepted the staff and turned away.

As she hobbled around to the backside of the stone to take care of morning matters, the stick made walking so much easier. She should have searched for something like this herself.

When she returned to the camp, she felt more like herself. There was much she could do to prepare for their departure this morning, but perhaps she should take over cooking the morning meal. After all, making food really *was* the woman's role. If she hoped to ride his horse today—as she would need to —she should offer this kindness.

She hobbled to the fireside, and he lifted his focus from the pot for only a quick glance. "Is the walking stick sturdy enough? I can find one thicker if that would help."

"No. This is right." Her tongue seemed to stumble over the words. Probably because she hadn't quenched her morning thirst yet. Not because this man's nearness affected her.

She motioned him aside. "I'll do the cooking." Her words sounded harsh. She hadn't meant for them to, but maybe a stern tone would make him step aside.

He didn't move, though, only used a wooden spoon to stir whatever was in the pot. "Do you have any camas cake left? I made meat stew. I know that's not normally a morning food, but it's so cold that I thought it would warm our bones for the day. Camas cake would go good with it. Stick to our ribs for the day's ride." His gaze shifted to her ankle. "If you're able to ride, that is. We could wait another day."

"I'm able." The words tumbled out as she shuffled to her pack. Easing down to her knees, she pulled out the bundle and shifted closer to the fire. The cake always tasted better warmed.

Silence slipped over them as they each focused on their own preparations. A small sound drifted from the bedding behind her, and Watkuese twisted to see. Pop-pank's furs stirred, revealing the girl's face. Her eyes stayed closed though, her expression relaxed with that peace that only came in sleep.

Warmth slid through Watkuese as she studied those sweet features. The nightmares that had plagued the child had finally lessened, allowing this peacefulness most nights. At least that part of the child's struggles had grown easier. If Watkuese could take away the rest of her pain...

"You have a good daughter." The deep tones of Hugh's voice rumbled in the still air, it's gentleness slipping through her.

She kept her focus on Pop-pank, but his words wrapped around her, clogging her throat and stinging her eyes. "She's everything to me." They were all each other had.

"Her father...?" His question came out halting. As well it should. Most men wouldn't bring up such a conversation.

And normally, she wouldn't want to share the details of her story with a stranger. But in these quiet morning moments, he felt more like a friend. She had no reason to withhold her history.

Turning back to the fire, she pulled the camas cake away from the warmth and reached for a knife to slice off chunks. "Both her mother and father died from the spotting sickness during the winter moon. Pop-pank's mother asked me to raise her as my own. She is my daughter now, the child of my heart. It's still hard for her though. Some days I think she wishes she had gone with her parents."

Why had she said that last part?

45

Because it was true, though she'd not even allowed her thoughts to form it.

As she kept her focus on the food, she watched the man from the corner of her gaze. For once, he wasn't watching her. But his brows had gathered, and he stirred his stew in a steady rhythm, his eyes glazed as though his mind lingered far away.

Then the knot at his throat bobbed. "It's hard to lose a good parent." His mouth closed and his throat worked again. He stopped stirring, though he continued staring into the stew. His words, the memories that must be planted in his thoughts now... Which parent had he lost? And how young had he been?

She shouldn't ask such a personal question, but she lived her life doing what others said she shouldn't. "Was it your mother or your father?" She kept her voice gentle. She only wanted to learn more of him, not bring pain.

He finally offered a quick glance. "My ma died giving birth to Louis." The corners of his eyes creased as though trying to smile, but only sadness cloaked his gaze. "She was a good woman. The best mother I could have asked for. You remind me of her, the way you are with Pop-pank."

An ache settled deep in her chest. She couldn't imagine a stronger compliment, but the sadness of both their situations took away the pleasure she wanted to feel. "I hope I can be what she needs."

Once more, he lifted his gaze, but this time his focus bore into her. "You've taken responsibility for her. You keep her fed and protected. You love her the way a mother should. It looks like you're exactly what she needs."

The intensity of his words, of his gaze, held her fixed. Had anyone been there to do those things for him? Her hand itched to reach out. To close the distance between them and cradle his face. What then? She'd always been bold. Spoken and acted as she wished without worrying about others' opinions.

But she didn't dare.

A sound from behind saved her from questioning her decision. When she turned, Louis sat upright in his bedding, hair mussed on both sides. When he saw her, he offered a sleepy grin.

She couldn't help but return the smile, even though her mind lingered on the man kneeling just beyond the fire.

CHAPTER 7

*H*ugh eyed the mountain rising before them, then glanced toward the sun, partway down its descent. Scaling that cliff would take at least half a day, probably longer. Then they would need time to descend the other side. Better to camp here and save that trek for the morrow.

He motioned toward a group of trees that would provide shelter. "We'll stop here for the night, then start up that mountain tomorrow."

"Alrighty." Louis nudged his mount forward toward the copse.

Mounted on his gelding, Watkuese didn't speak. He glanced up at her and saw the tension at the line of her jaw. Was she upset because they were stopping early? But the creases of pain beneath her eyes showed more. He couldn't see the injured ankle from this side of the horse, but the limb likely throbbed from hanging down all day. Camping early would be best. He needed to find water for her to soak the leg.

He and Louis worked quickly to set up camp, and the fact that Watkuese immediately sat on the ground to start the fire attested to her pain. Pop-pank ran back and forth between the horses and her mother, carrying supplies first, then gathering sticks and small branches. It didn't take long before she began to dawdle, spinning in circles and falling to the ground or building things from sticks instead of bringing them to her mother.

"Pop-pank." Watkuese's voice hummed tight with frustration. "Bring those branches here."

The girl answered in the Shoshone language they'd all been speaking, but the lazy cadence she used made it hard for him to decipher the words. Something about *later*.

"*Now*, Pop-pank." The snap of Watkuese's words brought Hugh's attention to her face, where tight lines edged her eyes. The pain probably shortened her temper. Yet a glance at Pop-pank showed the girl didn't even look up. Should he interfere on Watkuese's behalf? He had to.

But before he could speak, Louis stepped in. "Poppy, gather up all the sticks you can find here, and then you and Hugh can go to those other trees and look for bigger logs. You might even find some winter berries like we saw earlier."

The girl finally looked up, and her entire countenance brightened. Her teeth flashed in a grin that she aimed first at Louis, then turned on Hugh. "I will." She jumped to her feet and scooped up the sticks she'd been playing with.

The moisture dried in Hugh's mouth as he dropped his bedroll with the others. He was supposed to take the girl off on his own? By himself? Or...rather, just the two of them?

What if she expected him to talk and entertain her like Louis did? He'd disappoint her for certain. But at least walking to the distant trees should be safe enough. They weren't likely to encounter anything that preyed on humans, and as long as she didn't climb trees or rocks, she wouldn't fall. Surely he could manage to keep her safe, if not smiling the entire time.

Pop-pank was clearly excited about the prospect, as she nearly ran back and forth to her mother with branches. This would help Watkuese, giving her a few moments of peace while he kept her daughter busy.

He could do this for her.

"I'm ready. I picked up all the sticks here."

Hugh stared into the wide hopeful eyes turned up to him. He couldn't disappoint Pop-pank, not when the guarded look already lingered in her dark gaze. She was preparing herself for him to say no. Preparing herself to hide away behind her petulance. He knew exactly how that felt, how easy it became to don that protective coat.

So he nodded. "I'm ready."

With a wave to Watkuese, they set off. Pop-pank had to run two steps for each of his, so he slowed his stride. When the girl scampered ahead of him, he returned to his original pace. She'd probably stored up extra energy after being confined to a saddle most of the day.

They trekked along the base of the mountain, and Hugh's gaze wandered upward. Tomorrow they would have to scale that beast. He could make out a path partway up, probably a game trail, but beyond that, vertical cliffs and massive rounded boulders covered every part he could see. Would they find a path the horses could manage?

"What are you looking at?" The little voice tugged his attention back down. She was staring up at the peak as he had been.

He followed her gaze. "I was trying to decide which path we should take when we climb that mountain tomorrow." He pointed toward the faint markings of the route. "There's a trail the animals have made that goes a little more than halfway up. But I'm not sure which way we'll go past that. I guess we'll look for a way when we get there."

"The animals wouldn't stop halfway up, would they? We can find the rest of their trail to the top."

The girl possessed some common sense. When she looked at him with those pretty dark eyes, he couldn't help a smile. "I hope we can. The only problem might be if the trail was made by big horned sheep or goats. They're so good at climbing these mountains, they can go places the horses can't. I guess we'll have to wait and see."

She nodded, her expression so sober he almost smiled again. He nearly reached out to ruffle her hair but caught himself. Would that be too familiar? He knew nothing at all about little girls.

They'd nearly reached the trees, so he shifted his focus there. Firewood he knew far better than people. "Let's stack the wood here that we want to take back." He motioned to the edge of the grove.

They both set to work, and Pop-pank showed none of the sullenness she sometimes slipped into. But as he carried his second load to the pile, her silence seemed to grow thicker. He'd never associated little girls, or women either, with quiet. Was something wrong? Had he said the wrong thing and hurt her?

Brow creased, she worked with a sort of dogged determination. Something certainly seemed to have bothered her.

He scooped up a smaller stick near the stack for an excuse to linger there until she came with another handful. After tossing his load at the same time she piled hers, he spoke quickly enough to snag her attention before she turned away. "Is there something bothering you?"

A wary expression guarded her eyes, and she shook her head. But she didn't turn and walk away, just stood watching him.

Should he stoop down to her level? Or would that make the conversation feel awkward? He was too big an oaf to know how to handle children.

He didn't lower himself, but he did make his voice as gentle as possible. "If there's something I did or said, I'm sorry. I'm not always good with words."

The wariness in her eyes turned to a full scowl. "It has nothing to do with you."

He raised his brows at her sharp tone. He wasn't usually one to think of himself overmuch, but perhaps that was what he'd done here. Maybe she'd been walloped with a memory of her parents that brought on the sadness. He could well remember how that felt.

Even though he and Louis had escaped to the Heinrichs' farm after Ma died, the simplest things could raise a memory of her—waking to the scent of hay in the barn where he slept made him think of those times when he'd crept into her bed after a nightmare. She always kept the tick freshly filled, and somehow he'd learned to associate the scent of hay with the protection of her warm hugs. In those early days after her death, such memories would slam into him when he let his defenses down even a little.

Now, as he studied this dark-haired girl, he could see pain behind her barricade. Perhaps he could say something that might help. "I know things are hard for you. I'm sure you miss your ma and pa. The pain gets better, I promise." Though it never went away completely. "You're lucky to have your new mama, Watkuese."

The girl's chin jerked sideways as though he'd slapped her, and her eyes flashed. "She's not my mama."

Like a startled dear leaping through a meadow, Pop-pank spun and sprinted through the trees.

"Wait." A knot pulled tight in his belly. He'd bungled that one for certain.

He started after the girl, lengthening his stride into a brisk walk. Of course she might not want to think of anyone replacing the mother who raised her. He should've thought of that. Mrs. Heinrich had been like an aunt to him, but she could never have replaced his ma.

As Pop-pank's form became only a shadow among the trunks, he pushed into a jog. "Stop! Pop-pank."

If anything, the girl sprinted faster. Worry tightened his chest. She'd run away from Watkuese the night they'd left the village. Watkuese had never said why the girl ran, but he'd assumed Pop-pank was simply acting out, as some children were wont to do.

Had there been some kind of emotional argument with Watkuese that sent her fleeing? Or perhaps even a single word or memory that brought up the grief. Once or twice, he'd run as far and fast as he could to escape his heartache. He'd never been successful, but perhaps Pop-pank hadn't yet given up trying to outrun her pain.

He slowed to a walk but kept on her trail. She needed time to gather herself. Probably tears were already falling, and she'd be better off if she had a chance to finish the cry before he found her. If the girl knew the area, he wouldn't go after her at all. But he needed to make sure she was safe.

Following her tracks wasn't hard as he wove through the woods. She certainly wasn't trying to disguise her steps. When the trees ended, her prints continued on to a section of solid rock, like smooth boulders raised only slightly above the ground. He could spot the first several steps easily, for Pop-pank's moccasins had been damp. The tracks quickly disappeared, but he kept going in the line they'd set.

She had started up the base of the mountain at a slant that wasn't too steep yet. A few larger rocks where she could be hiding littered this slope. She must be tucked behind one of them, for he could see her nowhere in the open.

Still, the unease in his belly tightened to worry. Anything could happen to a child alone in this mountain wilderness. A single slip could send her tumbling down the cliff. She could break a limb. What if he didn't find her and she had to spend the night without furs or fire? If he lost the girl, how could he face Watkuese?

He *wouldn't* lose her. She had to be somewhere on the slope.

Yet, the stone underneath his feet made it nearly impossible to find tracks now. Was there something he was missing? He alternated between searching the ground and scanning the area around in case the girl popped out from wherever she hid.

Should he call for her? The farther he went without finding her behind any of the rocks, the tighter the angst inside him grew. "Pop-pank." He tried to keep his voice steady, no sign of anger or worry. The last thing he wanted was to scare her off.

He lengthened his strides to close the distance to the next boulders. How far up would she have gone? "Pop-pank." No little girl was tucked behind the rocks.

He paused and turned in a full circle, staring out over the landscape in all directions. He'd gone farther up than he thought. Cupping his hands around his mouth, he raised his voice. "Pop-pank!"

"Hugh?" The answer was not the voice he wanted.

Louis stood at the edge of the trees, watching him. "What's wrong? Where's Poppy?"

Frustration simmered higher in Hugh's chest. Now Louis would think he'd lost the girl, when really he had just been trying to give her time.

Then Louis would tell Watkuese. A new pain pressed in his chest. She would think him incapable. Irresponsible. Not good enough to spend time with her daughter.

And she would be right.

He yelled louder this time, not trying as hard to keep the panic from his voice. "Pop-pank!"

Louis strode toward him, and Hugh turned to glance once more up the mountain. More rocks and boulders covered the landscape farther up, but the girl couldn't have climbed that distance in the short time since she'd left Hugh's side. His gaze circled once more. He and Louis could each go in different directions around the side of the mountain. How could she have disappeared so quickly?

He turned his focus to his brother and stepped forward in long strides to meet him.

Louis panted as he came to a stop. "What's happened?"

"Pop-pank ran away from me. I followed, but she disappeared. She couldn't have gone any farther up the mountain, so we should spread out along the sides. You go that way. Check behind every rock and bush."

Louis gave a salute, and thankfully, didn't ask any more questions before jogging the direction Hugh had pointed. That left him to resume his own search. As he started to the left around the mountain, the distance seemed endless. Rocks and cliffs littered the incline. The girl could be anywhere.

He'd never felt more incapable.

A sting burned his eyes and the back of his nose, a sensation he'd not felt since the death of their middle brother.

The feeling wasn't welcome now either. He had to find her.

Charging forward, he ran as fast as he could manage on the uneven ground. With every step, every pounding heartbeat, he steeled his resolve a bit more. He would find this girl and return her to her mother. He would get them to the Shoshone village as fast as they could travel.

Then he would take himself far, far away, where he couldn't bring any more pain.

～

Watkuese swung forward as fast as she could manage with the walking stick supporting her injured leg. Perhaps she should throw the staff aside and ignore the pain so she could really run.

Pop-pank had disappeared again, she was almost certain

from the panicked calls drifting in the distance. If the girl had been hurt, they wouldn't be shouting for her, so she must be missing.

Why had she allowed her daughter to leave her sight? Hadn't she told herself the last time the girl disappeared in the night that she would never let her go again?

Hugh had been there that night too. He should have known not to let Pop-pank stray far. He should've known she might hide. Shouldn't he? Watkuese had never actually told him about this awful game her daughter had begun playing. This wasn't his fault.

It was hers. Pop-pank was her responsibility. She had to take better care of her.

But if he'd been watching more closely…

She hobbled out of the trees and slowed to take in the slope of the mountain rising before her.

Rocks jutted out everywhere—so many places her little girl could hide. Bile rose into her throat. How would they ever find her? Pop-pank would have to come out on her own, but what if she didn't want to? What if they couldn't convince her?

She fought back the burn of tears, blinking to clear her vision. She couldn't see either of the men, but from the sounds of their voices calling, they must have gone opposite directions around the mountain.

That left the slope ahead for her to search.

Her ankle throbbed as she started forward. Part of her wanted to succumb to the pain and drop to her knees already. But she couldn't. She had to look.

As she struggled over a section of uneven rock, a call sounded from her right.

"I found her." Hugh's voice rang from somewhere out of sight.

The terror choking her throat eased, and she finally drew a full breath. She started that direction. Was Pop-pank safe? He hadn't said she was hurt, but he hadn't said she was well either. The tangle in Watkuese's middle pulled tight again. This time she really wouldn't let her daughter out of her sight until they were safely returned to the village.

Two figures rounded a distant cluster of rocks—a tall, broad man and a girl who reached only half his height.

Pop-pank walked steadily beside him, no sign of injury. No happy lilt in her step, but no scowl and dragging of her feet either.

Watkuese paused to wait for them. Her ankle would no longer bear any unnecessary steps. By the time Hugh and her daughter reached her, Louis had approached from the other direction.

She focused on Hugh's expression. No sign he'd been panicked. He seemed as calm as ever. She had much to say to the man, but not here. Once they made it back to camp, she would find the right time.

She turned to her daughter and held out her arms. "I'm so glad you're safe. I was worried."

The girl didn't speak and didn't step into the hug Watkuese offered. Pain pressed in her chest. She only wanted to love this daughter. Why did Pop-pank keep throwing that back at her?

Watkuese hobbled forward and wrapped her arm around the girl anyway. Maybe the child needed to know how far her new mother would go for her.

To the end of the earth, my love.

Pop-pank held herself stiff at first, but finally sank against Watkuese's side to allow the embrace. Watkuese pressed a kiss to the top of her hair.

At last, she straightened and glanced from one man to the other. "Let's go back."

"I'll get Snowy for you to ride back." Louis looked to her for permission.

She shook her head. "We'll walk." As much as her ankle

protested, she would endure the trek. She needed to get her daughter back to that safe place and have a private conversation with Hugh. The man hadn't spoken a word since bringing Poppank back.

For some reason, that raised her frustration all the more. Had his relief stolen his voice? Or his shame for losing the girl? She had a suspicion something far stronger kept him distant, but she had no idea what. Would she ever understand this man?

CHAPTER 8

*T*he anvil pressed against Hugh's chest hadn't lifted.

He dropped his armload of firewood with the rest of the stack by the fire and stepped aside so Louis could do the same. On the way back to the campsite, they'd picked up what he and Pop-pank had gathered before her disappearance.

The tension lacing the air during their return had thickened when camp came into view. Watching Watkuese's hobbles had brought more pain to him with each step, but he well knew she wouldn't accept any assistance.

Now, she didn't sink down to rest on her furs, which meant she must plan to speak with him first. She'd settled Pop-pank there and was speaking to the girl quietly, likely giving strict orders as to where the child was allowed to go.

Then Watkuese straightened and swiveled on her good foot to face him. The glare in her expression shot all the way to his core. Her anger was justified—he'd been responsible for her daughter and lost the girl. But didn't Pop-pank bear some responsibility for disappearing? He'd been running after her, calling her name, and the child had only sprinted faster away.

"Come with me." Watkuese's voice held a low tension as she

charged past him, the walking stick propelling her forward. The walking stick *he'd* found and smoothed out for her.

He followed, working for deep, steady breaths to keep his own head level. He would hear her out, apologize for any wrong on his part, and be done with the matter.

She led him away from the few trees surrounding their camp and stopped by a boulder a dozen strides out. She turned and eyed him with an expression that made him want to take a few steps back.

He stood his ground.

"How did you lose my daughter?"

Everything about her—the fire shooting from her eyes, those accusing words that weren't true—made him want to tell her exactly whose fault this whole ordeal had been.

Pop-pank's. He'd only been trying to help. He'd not even wanted to take the girl off in the first place.

He mastered his anger into a tight voice. "I didn't lose her. She didn't like something I said and ran off. I went after her, and as you remember, I found her and brought her back." There. That should put her in her place.

Her eyes flared. "What did you say to her?"

A tiny flag of caution waved in his spirit, making him pause. But his words couldn't hurt her, could they? "I told her I knew it was hard to lose a parent but that she was lucky to have you."

Too late he realized how that statement sounded. The wash of pain shadowing her face showed the full impact of what he'd not intended to say. He'd been trying to pay her a compliment, to show that he thought she was an excellent mother. But telling her that those words had made her daughter run away...

"I'm sorry, Watkuese. That wasn't—"

She was already turning from him. As she hobbled back toward camp, the slump of her shoulders showed how much of her flame he'd snuffed out.

He stayed where he was. Better he keep his distance for a

while. *Forever* would be best for them, but he still had to get the pair over the mountains.

If only he hadn't agreed to the job. It had sounded reasonable —he'd wanted to set out for the mountains, and she needed someone to travel with for protection. Surely a host of other people from the Nimiipuu village would have been better companions, though.

From the trees surrounding the camp, Louis stepped out of the shadows. He eyed Hugh, but thankfully didn't say anything. Not yet.

As he sauntered forward, however, it wasn't hard to see his baby brother planned to speak. Louis usually had a knack for saying something to relieve the tension in a situation, but there couldn't be anything he might say now that would help.

When Louis reached him, he stood and stared up at the mountain, his manner casual. Several more moments passed before he spoke. "You figured out our route up that slope?" Apparently, whatever Louis meant to say would be especially hard to hear, for he felt the need for small talk beforehand.

Hugh gave a single nod. "I think so." Mostly. He'd work out the higher parts when they reached them.

Louis nodded. "I thought you might have." He finally turned to Hugh. "I'm sorry if I pushed too hard, sending you off like that."

That wasn't at all what he'd expected from his baby brother. An apology? An acknowledgment he might've been wrong?

Louis turned back to the mountain as he continued speaking. "Do you remember back when you used to help Jeb with the plowing?"

Louis paused as if he were waiting for an answer, but Hugh couldn't have managed one, not with the lump burning his throat. Louis was the only one who'd called Mr. Heinrich by his given name. Besides Mrs. Heinrich, of course. Louis had been their golden-haired treasure, the son they never had.

Hugh had brought him to the family when Louis was hours old, right after Ma's final breaths, in hopes that Mrs. Heinrich could nurse him. The couple had been wary at first, but it didn't take long for Louis's angelic face and sweet personality to win them over.

He'd been so grateful that they'd allowed him to stay on to watch over his brother. Sleeping in the barn had been far better than leaving Louis with strangers. Hugh had worked to earn his keep, whatever Mr. Heinrich asked. And yes, he well remembered plowing beside the man.

Mr. Heinrich had been nothing like Pa, never telling Hugh how much he did wrong or how lazy he was. Mr. Heinrich only encouraged, pointing out the good things Hugh did and noting ways to do them even better.

Those had been the bright spots of his growing up days. Seeing his brother so loved and nurtured had been one of the best parts. Exactly the kind of childhood Ma would have wanted for her baby.

He worked to pull himself from the memories. Louis had grown quiet, which meant Hugh had better pay attention.

His brother watched him, studying. Something in his expression reminded Hugh of the little boy he'd once been. When Louis spoke, his voice seemed caught in a happy memory. "Jed loved when you worked with him. I always thought you liked it to. I didn't think we'd ever leave that place."

Hugh shrugged, doing his best not to let Louis's words in. Those days were long gone. And Jed—Mr. Heinrich—*hadn't* enjoyed his company. That became clear later.

"Why *did* we leave?" Louis might have heard Hugh's last thought, or perhaps he'd spoken it aloud. Though Louis was trying to sound casual, the undertone of hurt came through in his voice. He crossed his arms over his chest. "I mean, it wasn't like Pa wanted us at home."

The reminder of their father helped him swallow down all

tender emotion. Pa certainly hadn't wanted *him* there. Louis maybe, though Pa was the only one who barely gave his youngest son a second glance.

It was time he was honest with Louis. Hugh steeled himself and met his brother's gaze. "It was my fault. I'm the reason we had to leave the Heinrichs' farm."

Louis's brows drew into a furrow. "That's not right. They loved you."

Hugh managed a small smile. Even subjected to Pa's drunken, iron fist those past few years, Louis was untainted. Uncolored by bitterness and the realistic view of the world that some might call cynical. He still believed the best in others.

Hugh had to be careful not to spoil that, though his youngest brother did need a bit more worldly wisdom. "They were thankful for my work. But when their daughters began thinking about sweethearts, the Heinrichs were smart enough to send me packing. I'm sorry that meant you had to go too."

Louis tipped his head, studying him again. "Did you do something to worry them?"

Hugh sent him a glare. "Of course not. I never touched either girl, rarely even spoke to them. I knew better than that."

"Then why would they want you gone?" Louis's gaze penetrated far deeper than usual, all sign of that little boy replaced by the man he'd become.

Hugh shrugged. "Knew I'd be trouble, I guess. Too much like Pa."

His brother snorted. "You're nothing like Pa, and people wouldn't think you were trouble if you put a bit of effort into showing them different. Learn more about them and let them know you. Show them you're a good man. Smile every so often. Actually let yourself care." He raised his brows to drive the point home.

But then Louis must have realized he was hitting far too close to the waistline, for he turned back toward camp. "I'm going to see how I can help. Sulk a while if you need to, then come try what I said."

The knot in Hugh's throat slipped down to his belly as he watched his brother walk away. What would a lad like him know of such things? Yet Hugh couldn't deny how much he wanted to grasp onto Louis's words.

You're nothing like Pa.

If only that could be true. The reality was that he looked almost identical to his father—he had as a boy, and he still had the last time he'd looked in a mirror. Even Pa had said so all those years ago.

More than his appearance, he was too prone to temper. The one time he'd lost himself in drink had come too easily. He'd enjoyed it so much that it scared him. But what happened after that had terrified him even more. They said the man hadn't died from Hugh's blow, that it was a heart condition that took his life the next day. But the coincidence...

He would never allow that to happen again. No matter what, he wouldn't end up like his father.

What else had Louis said? People would like him better if he smiled more and took time to get to know them. Took time to care.

He'd worked so hard *not* to let himself care or get too close to others. He was saving them from himself and making things easier on everyone when he left. Keeping his distance was necessary. Louis would learn that.

A thought occurred to him. Maybe he *could* be a bit more amiable. Smile every so often and talk a little more. He would never have Louis's charm, but he could at least try not to be ill-tempered.

Inhaling a deep breath, he nearly sent up a prayer for help. The thought stopped him short. He'd not prayed since Mrs. Heinrich listened to his bedtime prayers that last night. Until that day, he'd begun to believe God was real and that He might really care. Though He'd taken away Ma, the Almighty had brought him and Louis to the Heinrichs'.

But when Mr. Heinrich told him they had to go back home, that had felt like the final confirmation. God might be real, but He certainly didn't care about a boy who showed every sign of turning out to be the same bitter drunk his father was.

Forcing his feet forward, he headed toward the camp. As he wove through the trees, he made out the figures around the fire. Watkuese worked beside the flame, probably preparing food. Pop-pank sat nearby, her chin dipped and arms braced across her chest. Louis sat by the saddles at the edge of camp, wiping down the leather. For once, he wasn't in the midst of a conversation, regaling them with stories or asking questions or making jokes.

Louis's habits looked a bit different now, after what he'd said. Maybe his witty conversation wasn't so much to draw attention to himself as to help others feel special. That, in turn, made people like Louis better, but perhaps that wasn't his goal.

As Hugh stepped into camp, Watkuese eyed him, her expression as trusting as an injured wildcat's.

He sent her a smile. Hopefully it didn't look too forced. Surely practice would make that action a bit easier. He turned his focus to Pop-pank, and when he reached the girl, he dropped to his knees in front of her.

She regarded him with an expression too sober for a child, and that might be fear tinging her eyes. What did she think he would do?

He kept his demeanor as relaxed as possible and smiled again. "Pop-pank, I'm sorry if something I said made things harder for you. I don't always say or do the right things, but I never meant to hurt you or make you sad. I'll try to be more careful. All right?"

She hesitated but finally nodded—two slow bobs of her chin. Now his smile came easier. "All right. There's one thing I'd like to ask of you. I'm hoping we can make a deal. If I promise to be more careful about what I say, will you promise not to run off again? See, we're out in the mountains, and there are a lot of places that can be dangerous if you're not with someone to help you. We have to stick together out here. That's the only way we'll all get back to your village safely. Is that a deal?"

She rolled her lips in, her brows lowering as she contemplated his words. If she agreed, would she take the promise lightly? As much thought as she appeared to be putting into her response, maybe she really wouldn't disappear again.

At last she nodded. "A deal."

Hugh eased out a breath and grinned, then extended his hand. "Sometimes when men agree on something, they shake hands to show they'll both hold up their part. Shake with me?"

Now her lips curved in a reluctant smile as she reached out to place her hand in his. Her tiny grip disappeared in his massive paw, reminding him with sharp clarity how fragile she was. At six, her heart could break so easily. Though Louis'd had the benefit of the Heinrichs' devotion, he'd still felt the loss of their mother, though he never knew her. How much more must this child be grieving.

He shook her hand. When he released it, a memory slipped in. Back when they'd had to leave the Heinrichs', he'd made something for Louis to help cheer him up. A horse, stitched from a soft rabbit skin. The boy had been the same age as Pop-pank, and Louis had adored that toy, carrying it everywhere.

Would something like that help this child? It might not have as much significance given from a friend instead of a brother— or perhaps she didn't even think of him as a friend, but he'd work on that too.

Still, something special made just for her to love might comfort Pop-pank. The effort couldn't hurt, and it could possibly help.

CHAPTER 9

*W*atkuese shouldn't have been surprised when she awoke to Hugh making the morning meal again. As before, she slipped from bed and hobbled to a private place to take care of pressing matters, then returned to camp and found a place to work beside him.

Yesterday's time had started off awkwardly, what with all the tension from Pop-pank's escape the night before. But she still couldn't get the images out of her mind of him kneeling before her daughter, making the agreement with her that they would each do better. She'd never seen him so gentle as when he took the girl's small hand in his strong one. Even now, the memory formed a lump in her throat. She could no longer hold a grudge toward him for losing her daughter.

That was why she'd forced herself to help prepare the morning meal yesterday, and the longer they worked together, the more they slipped into a rhythm. He'd spoken more than usual, asking about the kinds of foods she and Pop-pank ate in their Shoshone village, what berries and roots grew in the area, what their home was like, and how often the village moved locations. Now that she thought about it, they'd covered a great many topics. As he'd asked questions, she'd talked at length, so many pleasant memories making the conversation easy.

Today, she would be the one to ask questions. Perhaps he wouldn't want to speak of his own life, but she could at least pay the compliment of interest as he had done.

As she lowered to sit beside the fire to help him, the welcoming smile he offered brought the same fluttering inside her that it always did. Especially since his grin came more often now.

His gaze flicked down to her injured ankle as she placed it in the most comfortable position she could find. The leg had throbbed much of the night, making sleep come in pieces.

"Is the swelling worse this morning?"

She glanced up at his face, where lines of concern drew across his brow. "It doesn't hurt." Not true exactly, but she didn't need to be coddled.

He laid down the spoon he'd been using to stir what he called mush. She'd positioned her leg away from him when she sat, but he rose and moved around the fire to kneel beside her foot. Part of her wanted to pull the limb back.

He didn't touch her, only studied her tall moccasin. The swelling was worse, that couldn't be denied. After the grueling ride up and down the steep slope, the new bruising had been enough to make her look away.

He glanced up at her. "Yesterday's ride was hard. Can I take your moccasin off? I'd like to check the skin and bones."

She swallowed. *No.* Yet, she nodded, her head not obeying her mind.

With the same care and tenderness he'd used when he took Pop-pank's hand, he tugged on the laces, loosening them until the sides of the moccasin spread wide. Her ankle seemed to expand as the leather did, and the release sent a pounding ache up to her hip.

She focused on Hugh's face to distract herself from it. His

strong features could hold the attention of any woman—that square jaw, the even lips, and those eyes, which didn't hide when he smiled. The round scar on his temple only added to the strength that cloaked him.

He slid the moccasin off her foot. His actions were probably gentle, but the pull on her ankle made her suck in a breath. She blinked to clear her mind, then forced out the question she'd been thinking of asking. "How did you get the scar?" She brushed the same spot on her own face.

He didn't look up, just studied the brackish skin of her ankle. "A cut from a glass bottle."

That murky answer gave her far more questions than she'd had before. The scar appeared to be a few years old, too fresh to be a childhood wound where he might have accidentally injured himself. So had he been hurt in a fight? In a battle with many, or only a single person? And where? Did she dare press for more details?

He brushed his fingers across her ankle, and she barely kept from drawing in another gasp. Not only from the pain but from the way her body reacted to his touch. She couldn't let herself even think about why. "How did it happen?"

His fingers shifted to the other side of her ankle, the lightest of touches, yet it felt like water almost too hot to stand—shocking, yet wonderful. Maybe her body would adjust to the feel of him in the same way it did with the water.

When he slid his fingers down the side of the aching limb, she had to swallow her reactions—all of them. She *had* to distract herself. He hadn't responded, so she would ask again. Anything to busy her thoughts. "You didn't answer my question."

At last, he straightened, and she could see his sigh, though she couldn't hear it. His eyes shimmered with something like pain as he met her gaze. "It was a fight over something of little consequence. I was drunk and an idiot. It's one of the things I most regret."

Her throat went tight, her mouth too dry to speak. She looked away from his gaze. She hated the drink that made men mean and too sure of themselves. She'd been relieved that none of Otskai's group of friends indulged in it, including these two brothers.

Had that only been a temporary abstaining while they stayed in the Nimiipuu village? She hadn't seen either of them drink the stuff since they'd been traveling together, so they must not have any with them. That made sense. They likely drank it up right away when they were able to trade for it.

"I've never taken a sip since that night, and I won't in the future either. I shouldn't have then." His words brought her focus back to his face.

Had he seen her thoughts in her expression? She'd never been good at hiding them. Nor should she. She had no need to pretend to be someone she wasn't. So she nodded. "That's good. The white man's drink is bad for everyone."

A sadness settled in his eyes, and his focus seemed to drift inward, as though his thoughts had gone far away. "You're right." The words came softly, as if they'd had to travel all the way back from the memories that had drawn him in.

What wrongs had the strong drink inflicted in his past? Did it have anything to do with the parents he lost? As much as she wanted to ask, that felt like prying too deep into his pain. What he'd already told her had appeared hard enough for him. Perhaps he would come to trust her and share those deeper parts.

No, what was she thinking? Already, they'd traveled halfway across the mountains. Once they reached the village, Hugh would leave and she'd likely never see him again. She wouldn't have the chance to know all his stories, to understand what shaped this man into the combination of hard and tender that now stared into her eyes.

Awareness slipped through her, awakening both mind and body. His own gaze sharpened. Darkened. His throat worked, drawing her focus down.

Down to his lips. Hadn't she just been thinking how perfectly even they were? Very perfect. What would it be like to kiss those lips? Though she'd lived twenty-six winters, she'd never kissed a man. What if she did? This once.

Just this one impulsive thing. She'd never shied away from an impulse before. Why start now?

He must have leaned forward, for the distance between them seemed much smaller now. She swallowed. Did she dare?

But she was already closing the last of the space. She knew nothing of kissing, save that the woman's lips met the man's.

So she closed her eyes and touched her mouth to his.

~

*H*er mouth was completely unschooled, yet her touch burned all the way through him. What was he doing kissing her? Even as the thought tried to nudge in, the fire he'd seen in her before ignited, and her lips melded with his.

She learned quickly. Could this really be her first kiss? The thought shuttered in his chest, pulling back the desire that wanted so badly to run free. He'd only kissed one other woman —one of the women who frequented the bar that single awful night. Her touch hadn't ignited him like Watkuese's did.

He couldn't be reckless with her. Perhaps the kiss itself was already reckless, but he wouldn't regret this amazing, impossible... It felt too good to find words for it.

But he had to stop. If he didn't, she might regret having ever touched him. Maybe she already wished she hadn't.

The pain in that thought gave him the strength to pull back.

She didn't go far, maybe because he was gripping her arms. Her heaving breaths matched his, and he closed his eyes to relish the final moment of nearness, the warmth of her breath on his face.

A tiny whimper from the direction of the bedding broke through the fog in his mind. He pulled back, but not as quickly as Watkuese did. She spun so fast, she might have snapped a bone in her neck.

Pop-pank's blankets stirred, but her face hadn't peeked above them yet. She hadn't seen then. He could hope.

Watkuese scooted away, darting one glance back at him before reaching for her walking stick. "I'd better see to…" Her words were lost in her effort to rise.

He might have helped her to her feet, except she appeared desperate to get away from him. Once standing, she grabbed up her moccasin and hobbled to her daughter, and the two exchanged quiet words.

He turned back to the corn mush he'd been preparing. As he stirred, the spoon scraped a burnt crust on the bottom. He'd left it alone too long.

Clearly, that wasn't the only thing he'd done wrong. When would he learn that, no matter how careful he tried to be, he would never manage to do the right thing?

Watkuese was wise to run away from him.

~

*W*atkuese avoided Hugh as much as she could that day, and the next morning too. Not because he'd done anything wrong, but because she'd been so… She couldn't even find the word for it. Not in the Shoshone tongue, the Nimiipuu, or any of the English she'd learned.

Not only had she started the kiss, but she'd thrown herself wholly into it. At last, she'd found the situation where it was *not* good to be impulsive. Did Hugh think her the kind of woman to throw herself at a man?

She wasn't. Not at all.

That had been one of the reasons she'd left her father's village. He'd lined up one warrior after another for her, and nearly paid the bride price two different times before she'd intervened. She would not be sold off against her will—not three winters ago and not now.

She'd made it clear to everyone around her that she wouldn't marry until she found the one who stirred her heart. The one who made her come alive in her deepest being, who made her long to be with him when they were apart, who cherished her, as Pop-pank's father had cherished her mother. Those two had been the model that she'd been looking for, though she'd not realized it until she met them.

Kimana had tried to interest her in White Owl, her husband's brother. She'd said he'd spoken to her husband about Watkuese. That he would love her with that same devotion.

Perhaps he would. He was a good man, she was fairly certain about that. But... Her mind always stopped at the *but*. Maybe when she saw him again, she would know for sure.

The scuff of a stone beside her mount pulled her attention back to the present. To the man she was trying to forget.

Hugh hadn't sought her out since the kiss either. She could imagine why. Maybe he worried she'd throw herself at him again. Yet didn't men want a woman who easily fell into their arms? Could he be that different from others?

"Looks like a wide river in that valley." The deep timbre of his voice rumbled through her. Clearly he was paying more attention to their surroundings than she was.

She squinted into the flat land below them. Trees lined what must be the river, and as she focused, she could make out snatches of white foamy water.

The trail steepened, which meant she had to focus on her

mount and the rocky terrain they descended. Every time she glanced up, the river below came clearer.

And closer.

When the ground finally leveled off, a gap in the trees revealed what Hugh must've already seen. This would be the widest river they'd crossed yet.

A swiftly flowing one. The rush that caused whitecaps must mean the water went deep. Hopefully not so deep that the horses had to swim.

But they weren't *all* riding horses. She glanced back to where Hugh walked behind her mount. Could this gelding carry them both through that water? Perhaps, if he didn't have to swim.

That would mean they would be sitting close together, pressed tight between the front of the saddle and the packs loading the gelding's rump. Her throat went dry even as her body reacted to the thought. Her heart raced as though she already leaned against him, arms wrapped around his waist.

Would he want that? She couldn't deny the connection that roared to life during that kiss. Was it always this way between a man and woman?

She couldn't let her mind traipse down that endless path again.

They reached the river far too soon. The animal trail they'd been following led to a path worn into a deep groove down the bank. Tracks from deer, sheep, and a host of other tiny feet littered the damp ground at the edge of the water.

She glanced at Hugh. He'd called himself a trapper. If he were alone, would he stop here and set up his snares? If he weren't determined to accompany her and Pop-pank across the mountains, he likely wouldn't even have come this far before stopping to trap.

Though studying the river before them, he glanced at her as though he could sense her watching him. "Mind if I ride with you? It looks deep, but I hope the horses won't have to swim."

She nodded. There really wasn't another choice, not without making a scene by asking to switch with Pop-pank. Though perhaps the girl would be safer riding with Hugh. He was the larger of the brothers, stronger most likely. A better swimmer? She didn't know. But that would insult Louis, and he'd been so kind. He had a way of cheering her daughter when the girl sank into her sullen moods.

Perhaps Watkuese could use the horses as an excuse to switch mounts with Pop-pank. But Hugh's gelding was stouter, the one best suited to carry two grown people.

She would have to ride with Hugh and do her best to ignore the way her body ignited at his touch.

If only that were possible.

CHAPTER 10

*W*atkuese glanced at Louis and Pop-pank as they prepared to guide their horse into the river. Louis carried his gun in one hand and the reins in the other, ready to lift the weapon high above the water. Her daughter, wedged between Louis and the packs, clutched his waist. She would be secure if the horse had to swim, wouldn't she?

Still, she couldn't resist a warning. "Hold tight, Pop-pank."

The girl glanced at her with a nod and a wide grin that lit her face, its warmth spreading through Watkuese. If only that smile never disappeared.

Hugh stepped up to his gelding's side and reached for the reins. Watkuese surrendered them and scooted back against the packs to allow him room to sit in front of her.

He landed in the saddle, bigger than she'd prepared for. Even when she scooted tighter against the bundles to allow him as much space as she could, his bulk seemed a solid mountain. She did her best not to feel his nearness, not to react to his touch. It didn't help that her mouth resurrected the memory of his lips on hers.

"Hold on." Hugh's voice rumbled low, his words clearly

meant only for her. When he nudged the horse forward, the sway of its gait forced her to obey.

She rested her hands on his sides. At least the thickness of his coat lessened the sensation of the touch.

Their horse fell into step behind Louis's, but her body was far more focused on the man in front of her than their surroundings. That was...until their mount's hoof splashed into the water. The sound pulled her from the stupor, and she blinked to focus on their crossing.

Ahead, Louis's horse—Snowy, its name was—had already submerged to its chest. They hadn't yet reached the area where the water rushed fastest, swirling around rocks in a liquid tempest.

Her belly tightened. Would the horses be able to avoid that area? Were there rocks beneath the surface they couldn't see?

Snowy plunged deeper into the water, then bobbed back up, her head straining as she swam. Pop-pank squealed, submerged to her shoulders in the icy liquid.

A scream rose in Watkuese's own throat at the sight of her daughter nearly buried in the water. Should she swim to her? But what could Watkuese do except add more weight to the poor struggling horse. As long as Pop-pank held tight to Louis, they should make it across. "Hold on!" Her voice cracked as she yelled above the noise of the rushing water.

Whether her daughter heard or not, all Watkuese could do was watch as the horse struggled through the churning water.

Then the gelding beneath her lurched, as though his feet dropped out from beneath him. She clutched tight to Hugh, panic welling in her throat. Frigid water closed around them, rising up to soak her coat, tugging her sideways.

She gripped harder, wrapping her arms as far around his middle as she could with the river trying to pull her away. The horse swam forward, fighting against the water. Hugh's strong hand clamped over her wrist, holding her firmly against his middle.

She couldn't be swept away now, not unless he was too. And she had a feeling this man, with those strong arms, excelled as a swimmer.

"Hold on to the reins too." Hugh's voice deepened to rise above the sounds around them. "In case we're separated."

Leather was pressed against her hand, and she gripped it, still keeping her arm firm against his middle. With him holding her so tightly, there was no way they could be pulled apart.

She peered around Hugh's shoulder to see how Pop-pank and Louis fared. Surely they'd reached shallower water by now.

Water splashed in her eyes, and at first, only Louis's head and shoulders appeared through the blur. She blinked to clear her view, gasping as a swirl of foam hit her mouth.

When she could finally see again, Louis's head came clear once more. She could finally make out the smear of black that must be Pop-pank's hair.

The black floated away from Louis, and her mind struggled to decipher what she was seeing. A glimpse of pale skin attached to that black made her heart stutter.

Pop-pank!

Before she could react or even scream, Hugh pulled away from her and plunged into the swirling water. His strong arms wove through the current, just as she'd suspected they would. But his fur coat seemed to slow him.

She focused on Pop-pank, and her breath clutched in her throat. Her daughter, so small and fragile, was being swept downriver like a leaf. Hugh's bigger body couldn't move nearly as fast.

"Swim!" Watkuese screamed to her daughter, willing the girl's arms to rise from the water and propel her toward the shore. Every part of her wanted to leap from the horse and swim to save the child. But Hugh was already on his way, and if he couldn't help her, Watkuese could perhaps reach her daughter from the shore.

She turned her focus to the horse. The gelding swam hard, but carrying her probably slowed him down. She kept her grip on the reins and added a thick strand of the horses mane, then pushed off the saddle. The icy water tightened her chest. Using her free hand to swim, she kept abreast of the animal.

With water splashing her face and her efforts honed on getting to shore, she could only hear what was happening with the others. Louis called out, but she couldn't decipher his words. No sounds reached her from Hugh or her daughter.

Her muscles burned, threatening to go limp. She'd never felt so helpless. If only there was a greater power she could call on for help. A hand that could sweep down and pluck Pop-pank from the perils of the water. She'd never spent time listening to the shaman carry on about all the things the sun god and the smaller deities required, so of course they wouldn't be willing to help her now.

Maybe the God of the white men would help Hugh.

At last, the horse jerked, and its neck rose up above the water as it found solid ground. She scrambled to climb aboard the saddle, having to use a stirrup to accomplish it. Her entire body trembled, but she couldn't let weakness keep her from Pop-pank.

Her daughter.

The gelding struggled out of the river, water streaming from its body. Their supplies would need to be dried out. Later. After she held Pop-pank safe in her arms.

And she *would* save her daughter, no matter what.

The moment the horse reached the top of the bank, she plunged her heels into its side, turning the mount downriver. A few trees and brush lined the bank, and she had to strain to see between them.

There. Ahead and about two horse lengths from the bank

floated a small black mass. She hadn't braided Pop-pank's hair that morning, so the tendrils floated freely. Her head simply bobbed in the current. Did she move on her own at all?

Help her. Please. She didn't know who she cried out to, maybe Hugh, or maybe his God.

As she guided her horse down the bank, she looked frantically for the man. His arms still carried him through the water, but not as fast now. Was he too tired? *Don't let him be hurt.* Surely his God would protect him.

At the edge of the water nearest Pop-pank, Watkuese jumped from the gelding's back. When she turned to run into the river, another figure stopped her short.

A man stood in the current, directly in the path of Pop-pank's floating body. A warrior, his form too familiar. And the pale owl feathers tied into his braids removed any doubt.

White Owl. Pop-pank's uncle.

Relief washed through her, and the dread knotting in her middle nearly made her sink to her knees there at the riverside. But she kept her feet somehow, hobbling along the bank to meet White Owl as he scooped up the girl and waded through the water to the shore.

Watkuese avoided looking at him, keeping her focus on her daughter. When he reached her, she extended her arms to take her child. Pop-pank's eyes were slitted open, her head laid back on his arm as though she were completely exhausted.

My daughter. When Watkuese tried to take her, White Owl shouldered past her, carrying Pop-pank to a level stretch of grass before he dropped to his knees and laid her on the ground.

Watkuese bent over her, stroking the wet hair from her face. "My sweet one, are you hurt?"

Pop-pank's face was as pale as the newborn babe of a white woman, but her eyes were open. She lived. Thanks be to whatever Deity had saved her.

They had to get her warm now.

Suddenly, the girl's eyes rounded, and her skin turned a greenish cast. She gripped the grass beside her, and Watkuese barely helped her turn before water spewed from her. More liquid than could possibly fit in such a little belly.

Watkuese rubbed her back. "There. You'll feel better now." She kept her voice low and soothing, careful to keep out any hint of the worry crawling through her. What if Pop-pank had swallowed something that made her sick? What if she'd struck her head on a rock?

Finally, the girl seemed to have little left inside her—neither river water nor strength. Watkuese helped her lay back down and stroked her face in as soothing a touch as she could manage. Pop-pank had begun to tremble, so Watkuese rubbed her arms.

"Is she hurt?" Hugh panted as he trudged up behind her.

She spun to him. In the shock of White Owl's appearance and her worry over Pop-pank, she hadn't made sure Hugh came out of the water unscathed. Louis stood behind him, holding both horses. The concern on his face repeated the question his brother had just asked.

She turned her focus back to Hugh. "She's cold, but I think she'll recover. What about you?"

He shook his head. "I'm fine." But the slight wince that accompanied his movement belied the words.

She would have to believe him for now, though. She had a daughter to care for and the child's uncle to face—a man who looked rather angry with her.

And maybe for good reason. She should have ensured Pop-pank's safety in the crossing, not worried so much about her own feelings toward a man.

She leaned over Pop-pank again to study her. Her skin had regained some of its color. She was staring at her uncle, perhaps trying to decipher whether he was real or a vision.

White Owl chuckled, then tugged a strand of wet hair. "You are surprised to see me. It's good I have come or the fish would be biting your fingers." Though his tone was teasing, the glance he shot Watkuese held no lightness.

She should have guarded her daughter better, that she knew, but it was not this man's place to scold her. Though he may be Pop-pank's blood relative, her parents had entrusted Watkuese with her raising.

"Where did you come from?" The girl finally seemed to believe her eyes, and eagerness sounded in her voice.

"Our village. I came to find you and Watkuese and bring you home." Once more, he sent a look up to Watkuese as he spoke. This one was harder to decipher.

But if he thought she would cow to his censure, he would be disappointed. She raised her chin. "That's where we're going. You didn't need to come after us. I know where the winter camp will be."

He gave a single nod. "We will go there together."

Then his focus lifted to Hugh, and tension stretched the air. She straightened and glared from one to the other. She hated when men acted like bull buffalo, stamping and sniffing to prove who would win the herd. Better she take control of the situation.

First she turned to Hugh. "This is White Owl, Pop-pank's uncle." Then to the newcomer. "Hugh and Louis are brothers, friends of my cousin from the Nimiipuu village. They've been traveling with us."

That was all White Owl would get from her now. She turned back to Hugh and Louis. "We should make camp. A fire is needed to dry everything."

Louis finally spoke. "There's a pile of ashes near where we crossed. Looks like others have camped there before."

"That's good." She reached for Pop-pank's arms to help her up, but White Owl nudged Watkuese aside.

"I will carry her. She is weak still."

Watkuese allowed him to lean down and pick up the child,

but she walked by his side in case Pop-pank needed her. The girl wrapped her arms around her uncle and snuggled close.

A niggle of envy worked through Watkuese's chest. There had been a time Pop-pank would do the same with her, and she missed that warm sweetness so much. Would they ever be close again?

Hugh took his horse from his brother, and they all filed wearily upriver to the campsite. The air still hummed with a tightness that made her head ache, especially when she saw the looks the men sent each other. These glances weren't so much like bulls posturing, but they held definite distrust. Perhaps she could understand why White Owl might be concerned to see her and Pop-pank traveling with two white men, but he should give her the respect of believing she would only do so if the men were trustworthy.

Watkuese wrapped a fur around Pop-pank and sat her near the ashes from past fires. She planned to kindle the fire herself, but Hugh knelt over the spot with tinder and fire starter.

As he began arranging the bits of bark, he glanced at her and her daughter. "You two keep each other warm until this grows big enough to put off heat."

Watkuese settled beside her daughter and pulled her onto her lap, tucking the fur closer, then wrapping her arms around her. She rocked gently, and Pop-pank rested her head on Watkuese's shoulder. Her heart nearly melted from the warmth coursing through her. This was the version of her daughter she missed so much, loving and tender. Not burdened with grief that pressed in, doing its best to choke them both.

She had to find a way to help Pop-pank work through the pain to return to this sweet self all the time. If only she knew how.

CHAPTER 11

a battle raged inside Hugh as he nurtured the flames of their campfire.

Pop-pank's uncle.

The man had come to retrieve his niece—and her new mother as well. The proprietary way he'd taken over made that clear—along with the smitten looks he'd sent Watkuese when she wasn't looking.

Those glares he turned on Hugh, and even Louis, made it clear he didn't approve of her traveling companions. Would the man try to take Watkuese and Pop-pank away on his own? If Watkuese felt comfortable with this White Owl, perhaps Hugh and Louis should say farewell and start trapping as they'd first planned. Leave this blood relative to see them through safely. He certainly looked capable, in the prime of his strength.

For that matter, Hugh and Louis could stay camped right there. With all the tracks they'd seen, this area might keep them busy for the entire winter, or at least a long stretch of it.

But the thought of watching his girls ride away with that stranger churned bile in his belly. They weren't *his* girls, not really, but they felt that way. He'd been responsible for protecting them. Could he now turn off that protection like water smothered a candle's flame?

He'd never been able to do that before. Once he set his mind to look after someone, he could never really stop. He might go away for a time, but he always came back. Perhaps he should've remembered that before he'd agreed to take on this role.

He rose, doing his best to tamp down the anger inside him. Frustration with himself only. He never should have allowed himself to get into this predicament. He strode toward the horses. He needed time to cool off, to gather himself and make a plan before he tried to be sociable.

But as he rounded Snowy's head, Louis's rump appeared before him. The sigh that slipped out was a much better response than the frustration mounting inside. Louis straightened from where he'd been bent over to examine one of his mare's hooves. "I think she—"

His words halted when he caught sight of Hugh's face, and his brows rose. "Did you pick a fight with someone? Or are you planning to?"

"Neither. Came to check the horses." Why did his brother so easily assume the worst of him? "I'm being amiable, just like you said to do."

One of Louis's brows rose higher than the other. "As amiable as a wounded grizzly."

It seemed this wasn't the best place to cool off. Perhaps somewhere less crowded. He spun and headed deeper into the trees.

"Come back." Louis's chuckle only made the situation worse. "Hugh. Come back." Now he was laughing so hard he snorted.

Hugh paused and turned a glare on his brother. Louis had a hand clamped around his middle to hold in his belly laugh. He finally stopped chortling, but he couldn't quite wipe the grin from his face.

Hugh had seen that look so many times. Somehow, Louis

had managed it even as a baby barely able to sit up. That almost-contained laughter that made you want to tickle him until he released it in full—or at least until he told you the funny so you could join him. How did Louis manage to stay so innocent—so good—when he'd come from the same sire Hugh had?

Somehow, Louis had only taken on Ma's traits. Their mother had been able to smile in that same way, though hers had faded so much there at the end. Louis was a reproduction of her in all the good ways, even her appearance, with his fair hair and startling blue eyes.

The one thing God had done well in that awful last day when He took their mother was to bring Louis into the world with nothing of Pa in him.

"I'm sorry." After a final laugh-snort, Louis managed to form a serious expression. Mostly. "How's your head?"

Hugh struggled to pull himself back to the present. Though his skull still ached from the rock he'd struck in the river, he would recover. "Fine." He resisted the urge to reach up and touch the bump on the back of his skull.

"How's Poppy?" Louis nodded toward the campfire.

"Cold and wet and tired. I think she'll be better once she warms up." And happy to see her uncle. He wasn't ready to talk about that man, though.

"The uncle appeared to be a surprise. Is he traveling on with us?"

It seemed Louis would force the topic. If they were going to part ways with the girls here, Hugh should go ahead and tell his brother. But was that really what they should do? Maybe Louis would want a say in the decision. After all, he was old enough to have a voice in where he went and what he did.

Hugh aimed for a casual tone. "I think the uncle plans to take them the rest of the way himself. It might be best if we stay here and start trapping. The animal sign looks promising."

Luis's jaw dropped in that annoying look that said he was

questioning Hugh's ability to think rationally. "You would abandon them?"

He spun to fully face his brother. "Not abandon. He's Pop-pank's uncle. And he clearly thinks they're both his to protect."

Louis finally closed his mouth, but then he raised his brows. "But they're not. Are they." That last bit definitely wasn't a question. "You promised to take them safely across the mountains. You promised to protect them both. You don't really want them to go on without us, do you?"

"It doesn't matter what I want." His baby brother had developed a bad habit of poking his nose where it didn't belong.

"But it *does* matter that you gave your word." Louis's voice softened, but the truth in his statement cut like a freshly-honed blade. "The brother who raised me, who protected me, would see them all the way to their village. You're a little different now, but I think that fellow is still inside you."

Was he different? Of course. He'd learned a few things from life. But did that mean he'd become a worse person? Better at ducking the punches life threw, sure. At keeping himself from getting hurt. He accomplished that mostly by maintaining his distance.

But he was trying to do better. He'd been asking questions and listening, and he'd enjoyed the conversations so much more than he'd expected.

Louis was right. Hugh had given his word to take Watkuese and Pop-pank home. Even if the entire village came to travel with them, he would fulfill his promise.

"Besides..." One corner of Louis's mouth tipped. "I'll bet if you ask the lady, she'd rather have you than the other fellow."

With a scowl at his brother, Hugh slammed the lid on that thought before it could slip in and fester. Turning, he started back toward camp.

White Owl had built a two-sided structure near the fire, which would be a nice windbreak for the girls. Did he plan for them all to stay here more than one night? Watkuese surely wouldn't consider the thought.

Pop-pank lay where she'd been sitting before, and when he drew near, the gentle rise and fall of steady breathing proved she slept. He crouched beside the girl to study her. Those dark strands of hair had dried stringy, and her skin was still a bit pale. But she looked so much better than when she'd first been pulled from the river.

If only he could have reached her sooner—or at all. But he was thankful White Owl had been there to pull her from the water. No matter how he felt about the man, it seemed they both cared about this little girl.

Voices drifted from the other side of the shelter, and he glanced up. Watkuese's tone was low and insistent. Then White Owl spoke, his deep voice ringing loud enough to make out the words.

"You should marry me. You must. It's best for you both. I'll be a good husband to you and will raise my niece as my own. I won't let her forget the parents who loved her."

Hugh couldn't breathe as he waited for Watkuese's response. Did they know he was near? Eavesdropping or not, he had to hear whether she agreed. Should he still travel on with them if she said yes? As hard as that would be on his heart, perhaps his presence would be needed even more if the two were promised to each other. He'd get to be their chaperone. What a privilege.

"I'm glad you will speak to her of the parents who birthed her and loved her. I will do the same. But you don't need to be her father to do this. Nor do I have plans to marry."

Hugh's relief came out in a sigh he barely kept quiet.

"Why should you be alone and without protection when I am willing? I will be a good husband and you will be a good wife." White Owl's voice had taken on more of a pleading tone.

"You are *willing*? Perhaps I will not be as good a wife as you think. We'll never know. I will *not* marry. But don't worry, I'm not alone, I have Pop-pank. And I've been trained with weapons. I can protect us both." A bit of steel edged Watkuese's voice.

Hopefully, White Owl realized he would only hurt his cause if he pushed further. But part of Hugh silently urged the man to keep pushing.

Watkuese had said *no*. She didn't plan to marry this brave. No matter that they seemed like the perfect little family from the outside.

She'd said no.

Did that mean Hugh stood a chance with her? He shouldn't want a chance, though. He was too much like his father, not nearly good enough for her. Despite that, at least she was still available. Maybe if he worked hard enough, he could become the kind of man she needed.

CHAPTER 12

*W*atkuese had forgotten how much White Owl reminded her of his brother, Pop-pank's father. She watched him now as he sat across the little clearing where they camped, Pop-pank perched on the log beside him, chattering about her summer in the Nimiipuu camp. Though she'd seemed tired most of the day, having her uncle's attention seemed to have brought the child back to life.

White Owl leaned over and cupped his hands around Pop-pank's, showing her how to make the sound of a duck by blowing into his hands a certain way. Watkuese could almost see Yagaiki in his place, lovingly teaching his daughter.

The brothers had only possessed a few common features—the same sharp chins, the same high arching brows. But their mannerisms were so similar. White Owl didn't speak as much as his older brother had, but they were both gentle. Quiet. Perhaps marrying and raising a child had drawn Yagaiki out.

Why did Kimana and Yagaiki have to die so young? Why must Pop-pank's tender heart be so bruised? It seemed a wound too great to heal. Too injured for Watkuese to make whole again.

"I brought water for you to soak your ankle." Hugh's light touch on her elbow brought her around as much as the rich timbre of his voice.

She stared into his face, letting herself linger and enjoy the way her heart beat harder at his intensely attractive features. The way emotion clogged in her throat as she sank into his gaze. She wanted to lean into him, to feel his strength around her. To rest in him.

She couldn't. There were others around—her daughter and White Owl especially. Hugh and White Owl had been casting each other wary looks all day, so she couldn't do anything that might propel the tension into something far worse. But that didn't stop her body from longing for his touch.

Instead, she smiled her thanks, then gripped her walking stick tighter and hobbled toward her place by the fire and the pot he'd positioned there. She'd stopped using the walking stick yesterday after White Owl came, but after the long day in the saddle, her leg had swollen again, and the ache pulsed through her.

She eased down onto the furs she would sleep on, then settled her foot in the water. This pot was large enough for the liquid to come up above the worst of the swelling, but it would have been heavy to carry.

She glanced over to where Hugh scraped something in their other pan by the fire. "How far did you have to go for water?" They'd had to make camp on the side of the mountain.

"Found a small spring halfway between here and the valley. The horses needed a drink too." He was a good caretaker, this man. Willing to do whatever was necessary to make sure those in his charge had everything they needed, whether they be horse or troublesome females.

"Thank you. This helps."

He finally glanced up at her, his eyes dancing as one side of his mouth tipped up. "I suspect your ankle is nearly numb already. As cold as it was today, that spring felt close to iced over."

She couldn't help but match his grin. "Perhaps." She already couldn't feel parts of her foot, but that was a welcome change from the throbbing.

Using the tip of his knife, he flipped what looked like meat in the pan.

"What can I do from here to help with the food?" She should be making the entire meal, not sitting back and watching.

A line creased his brow as he shifted the meat inside the pan. "This is all I have, actually. It's a good chunk of elk, should be enough to fill us. I'll do some hunting first thing in the morning. There wasn't much game around the Nimiipuu camp, so my supplies are low."

She reached for her own pack but had to crawl to grasp it. Once she settled again with her foot in the water, she unfastened the tie and pulled out a bundle of baked camas root. "I have plenty of this. My cousin let us help harvest her family's plot."

After pulling out enough for them all, she handed the food over to Hugh. Pop-pank had developed a taste for the camas that was a Nimiipuu stable, so Watkuese had spent much time preparing them, letting the roots bake for days so they'd be sweet and full of rich flavor.

Hugh also seemed to appreciate the way she cooked them. She hadn't missed the way he devoured the baked camas when she offered them in a meal.

While the meat cooked and the roots warmed close to the coals, silence settled over them. Sparks popped within the fire, and the low hum of the blaze wrapped around her like a comfortable blanket. Warm and familiar.

"You must have good friends with the Shoshone to want to go back there instead of staying with your family." Hugh's words didn't feel like prying. Perhaps they might have once, but the more she'd come to know the man, the more closeness seemed to grow between them.

For that reason, she gave thought to his question, which he hadn't really voiced as a question. "I suppose I do. None so dear as Pop-pank's mother was. But the women have accepted me. They're good people, kind and hardworking."

He lifted his gaze again, brows rising. "Kind and hard-working seems an apt description for the camp we left too."

She nodded. "They are." How could she explain that she still felt so controlled among those people? Though her father had no authority in the Nimiipuu camp she'd slipped away from in the night, he still reigned as chief in the village a half day's ride to the south. She could feel his presence in each place. Maybe it was the river that bordered both villages that made them feel so similar. She had to attempt to explain that to Hugh without distorting the situation.

"I have family in both of the Nimiipuu camps. Being so near them all, especially with my father being chief in the southern camp, I'm never quite free there. I prefer to make my own way, which the Shoshone allow me to do." She couldn't stop the way her gaze darted to White Owl, who sat too far away to hear their conversation. He wasn't quite as willing to allow her to make her own choices. Had he asked her to marry him merely because of Pop-pank? That seemed the most likely reason.

Hugh followed her gaze but then dipped his focus back to the food as he flipped the meat once more. Thankfully, he didn't remark about the brave who still sat beside her daughter, now sharpening the blade of his knife. "I didn't realize your father was a chief. Mine was no one special, but I can understand your desire to be on your own."

A hardness had crept into his voice, and now he stared into the leaping flames. Pain drifted from him, something so strong she could almost touch it. She wanted to draw him close and cradle him in her arms. To soothe away whatever had hurt him.

She kept her voice soft, as gentle as she could. "You told me of your mother, but not your father. Did he die also?"

One of his hands slipped into a fist. Maybe he didn't even realize the action. His thoughts still seemed so far away. "He passed a few years ago. He was...not a good man. Drank too much."

That seemed to be all he planned to say, but it explained much. Like why he'd been so adamant before that he no longer indulged in strong drink. She'd seen what awful things people did after consuming it. How it changed them completely. She'd always been grateful her father opposed it in their village.

But if Hugh's pa acted like the drunken men she'd seen, how much had he endured at the man's hands? And how much of that had formed him into who he'd become today? He seemed to have taken on the opposite of the things he'd watched and endured, at least when it came to the drink.

Had his father abandoned his family when strong drink consumed him? That might be why Hugh had become such a protector and caretaker.

As she glanced from the pot of water he'd brought for her to soak her leg, up to the man himself, so much became clear. He was a better man than she'd even suspected. Stronger—and he used that strength to help others.

This new insight felt like a gift, one she was fairly sure he didn't offer others. It made her want to give him something in return, a bit about herself.

"My father didn't indulge in strong drink. In fact, he didn't allow it anywhere in our village. When traders would come with the stuff, he sent them away at the point of his poison arrows. That was the way my father ruled—still does, it seems. When he speaks, he expects his commands to be followed. And the entire village obeys him. I don't think they follow him out of fear—not most anyway. But I have never been able to stomach blind obedience."

Hugh was watching her, the interest on his face clear, but with no judgment. "Is that why you left? He commanded you to do something you didn't want to?"

She shrugged. "Not one specific command. He'd been trying to marry me off to half the warriors in the camp. I knew I had to leave. A group of Shoshone from Kimana's village came for trading. They were kind and there were women in the party, so I believed I would be safe. When they left, I sneaked away with them."

His brows rose, and she knew exactly what he must be thinking. She'd not had the courage to announce her leaving, to give a proper farewell. She raised her chin. "I knew if I told them of my plans, my father would try to stop me. It was best I leave quietly. Best there not be a fuss."

He regarded her for a long moment, his scrutiny so intense she wanted to squirm. But she didn't.

"Did he come after you?"

She gave a single nod. "I told him I was determined to leave. He finally accepted my words and returned to his village."

The corners of Hugh's mouth tugged, though she couldn't quite read the expression in his eyes. Not humor. Perhaps something grim. "You're a strong woman, Watkuese. One day I'd like to know what made you that way."

He turned from her to the source of the approaching voices, but she couldn't push away his words so easily. Why did there have to be a reason for her strength? She simply didn't want to be controlled—she wouldn't be. She'd always been determined, and the things she'd seen as a girl had proven she was right.

Would that story satisfy Hugh's question? Perhaps if she could speak of it, but she couldn't. She couldn't relive those days.

Not even for him.

〜

*T*his rabbit's fur should be perfect.

Hugh pulled the knot tight to fasten the animal to his string, then strode toward camp again. They'd decided to spend the morning in this area for Pop-pank to rest and him to do some extra hunting. His trek had been successful—so much so that he'd have to go back with his gelding to bring the deer and sheep carcasses. They would provide enough meat to last the rest of this journey and beyond. He could even leave food for Watkuese to eat while she settled in the Shoshone village.

Who would hunt for her after that? Probably White Owl. The man seemed determined to claim her as his. In fact, he acted as though she and the girl already belonged to him.

Hugh tried to push down the anger that always rose when he thought of the man. Watkuese had refused to marry him. Why couldn't the brave except that?

And why did it matter so much to Hugh?

He shouldered through the flimsy branches of a cedar shrub. The whole situation shouldn't bother him so much. He had to detach himself. It wasn't as if he could truly have a future with Watkuese.

One unintentional kiss, sure. But their lives moved in separate directions. She was settled with her daughter to raise and spoke a language he'd just recently become fluent in. He was a roaming trapper who was too much like his father. Strong and too quick to temper. Though he would never again drink willingly, there was too much chance he might slide down the path that had ruined his pa.

And he couldn't impose that on any woman or child, especially not one he loved.

Not that he loved Watkuese, but he certainly admired her more than any other woman he'd met. Not just her looks, though they were considerable. Her spirit, her devotion, her endless strength to accomplish her goals, even while suffering from deep pain. The way she'd taken Pop-pank as her own and worked so hard to help the girl through her grief—all these showed the beauty of her heart.

Only a patch of trees separated him from camp now, and men's voices drifted from that direction. He listened for Louis's relaxed cadence. That was a French accent—speaking the French language, but not in his brother's tone. Did they have visitors?

Every nerve within him stood on alert.

One voice rose above the rest in a sharp bark. Then a grunt sounded. Pain.

Hugh dropped his catch and reached for his rifle as he shifted between the trees. He had to be careful where he aimed though. That camp contained too many people who mattered to him.

He bent low and quieted his stride and kept moving as quickly as he could manage in that position. The voices had dropped to low murmurs, so quiet he couldn't make them out.

But as he slipped from behind one trunk to the next, he finally caught sight of the source of the voices. A dark-haired man stood tall next to the campfire, and both his rough French words and the bushy beard showed he wasn't from one of the tribes.

He turned from speaking to another man, who was crouched beside their packs. "Where's the rest of it?" He barked the question to someone on the ground at his feet, then he landed a hard kick.

That same grunt from before sounded, fueling a surge of anger inside Hugh.

He shifted just enough to see that it was White Owl on the ground taking the brunt of the man's anger. Where were Louis and the girls? Had he taken them to safety?

But another figure lying beyond the fire made Hugh's lungs freeze. Louis lay facedown, unmoving.

CHAPTER 13

*P*anic welled within Hugh, swirling with his anger until rage sluiced through him. If they'd killed his brother...the only family he had left. The one who truly deserved to live...

He returned his focus to the strangers. The man crouching by the supplies was rifling through Hugh's own pack. Whatever they were looking for, they wouldn't find much of value in there. A leatherbound journal, a bullet mold, a sack full of bullets, and spare parts for the gun. Those belongings might bring a little in trade, but not enough to justify taking lives.

Hugh focused on the dark-haired man who stood over White Owl. He glared at the brave, and Hugh allowed his gaze to dip just long enough to see blood dripping down the Indian's face. His shoulders moved to show he still breathed, though his eyes were closed.

His attacker looked toward the far end of camp, and Hugh followed his gaze. He sucked in a breath. A third man stood just inside the tree line, rifle aimed at two figures a half dozen strides away from him.

Watkuese clutched her daughter, tucked partway behind her. Both seemed frozen midbreath, eyes locked on the barrel pointed at them. No fear showed on Watkuese's face, only watchfulness.

But Pop-pank. Her eyes rounded in more terror than any child should have to feel.

A new rage flooded him. He had to be wise about this. One man against three. The attacker standing over White Owl gripped a rifle. The fellow rooting through the packs held a pistol loosely in his hand, which wouldn't be as powerful or accurate. But at such close range, it could kill.

The varmint with his rifle aimed at the girls was by far the worst threat. Hugh had to stop him before he pulled the trigger. Would the lowlife shoot a woman and child without provocation? Surely Watkuese wouldn't do something to draw the man's ire. Not with her daughter in danger.

Hugh tightened his grip on his gun, but from this angle, he didn't have a clear shot at the man. And he would have only one chance.

As he eased over to the next tree trunk for better aim, the man who was crouched by the supplies pushed one of the packs away from him. "Nothing. Not even an empty flask." So much disgust filled his voice.

A flask? Had they come seeking whiskey? Drunken cads. They would risk innocent lives to feed their addictions? If that was the case, these men were more dangerous than he'd suspected. There might be another motive for their actions though.

Pressing himself against the new tree, he positioned his rifle and took aim. When he shot this man, he wouldn't have time to reload. He'd have to charge in with the empty gun and his hunting knife. And he'd have to be quick, before the other two could take action with their own weapons.

God, if You're up there, protect these innocent lives.

With that prayer rolling through his mind, he aimed at the man facing off with Watkuese and pulled his trigger.

Everything happened in a blur. From the corner of his eye, he saw Watkuese glance his way just as his finger tugged the trigger.

Her assaulter noticed too and spun toward Hugh. Even with the movement, his bullet struck hard enough to throw the fellow backward.

Hugh didn't have time to see how badly he was hit. "Run, Watkuese!" He charged forward, whipping out his knife and raising it toward the man standing over White Owl.

The fellow had turned his gun to aim at Hugh, but Hugh ignored the barrel and closed the final stride to plunge his blade into the man's chest. Bushy Beard blocked him with the gun in a movement so fast Hugh barely saw the flash of metal. His blade struck the barrel, and the force of his launch slammed through his shoulder as he stumbled backward.

Bushy Beard raised the rifle to shooting position again just as the man who'd been digging through the supplies appeared at his side. He wouldn't be as big a threat as the loaded rifle.

And Hugh wouldn't go down until they forced him.

Ducking below the aim of the gun, he charged forward, ramming his shoulder just below Bushy Beard's waist.

The gun exploded above him as he knocked the man backward. The entire world boomed and vibrated, knocking his senses into a whirlwind.

Even as his vision spun from black to flashes of white, he struggled to get his feet underneath him. Another body slammed into him, pushing him sideways. Something hot seared his leg, and hands closed around his throat.

He kicked the burning leg toward his opponent and grabbed at whatever he could reach. One hand found hair, the other flesh. A face.

He knew where the target was now, so he drew back and

used the force of his brute strength to plow a fist where it would hurt.

The man screamed, and the hands at Hugh's throat loosened. He shoved the stranger off.

His vision had finally settled enough for him to see his assailant roll away—even as the second man charged. Hugh brought his foot up just in time to halt the advance and shove that stranger back too.

Too much energy roared through his veins for him to feel any injuries yet. He had to get a weapon. Had to secure these no-goods.

He sprang to his feet and glanced around for one of the rifles, keeping the two men moaning on the ground in clear view. He was pretty sure neither were incapacitated. They had probably stayed down because they realized they wouldn't win the fight.

A blow slammed into the back of his skull, whipping his head forward with an explosion of pain. Light shot through his vision as darkness threatened to close in.

His hands and knees struck the ground, and he barely managed to keep from going all the way down. With every bit of strength he had left, he pushed back the blackness. He couldn't let these murderers win.

A roar sounded above him. At first it seemed to come from inside his scrambled mind. But then a melee of bodies swung in every direction.

Hugh pushed himself up to his knees. He might not manage to stand yet, but he had to see where the enemies were.

He barely had time to duck as Bushy Beard came flying toward him. In that half a heartbeat, he'd seen the face of a fierce Indian warrior behind the man, blood streaming down his face. He'd known White Owl likely possessed the training of a warrior, but rage flared in the brave's eyes as he slammed the butt of a rifle into the man who'd held the girls at gunpoint. Mayhap with that very weapon.

Bushy Beard's foot struck Hugh's ear as he tumbled, sending another round of dark and white flashes through his sight. He blinked hard to clear them once more. He'd never been so thankful to possess his father's fortitude against pain as he was now.

Looking up again, he spotted the man who'd searched the packs—on his feet with a knife poised to plunge at Hugh. Hugh had no weapon of his own and no time to search for one, so he tensed to roll away at the last second.

Before he had to act, White Owl lunged forward, the gun swinging like an ax. He struck the man at the base of the neck, who crumbled as though his bones had turned to liquid.

As much as Hugh would like to simply watch White Owl dispatch these brigands, he had to help. He turned, and the wince was impossible to hold in as pain shot through his head again.

Bushy Beard still lay where White Owl had thrown him. The man who'd been digging through the packs still crumbled from the blow with the rifle hilt. The one who'd threatened the girls knelt on the ground clutching his belly. Bent all the way forward, his forehead rested in the dirt. His chin turned enough that he could glare at White Owl through one good eye. The other had already swollen shut, maybe from Hugh's fist.

White Owl stepped toward the man, rage in his eyes, but Hugh reached out to stop him. There had been enough killing. Perhaps they could find a better way to end this than with more bloodshed. He wasn't near enough to reach the brave, and before he could speak, White Owl reached down and grabbed the stranger's arm.

Instead of slamming the rifle into his skull, a blow that would surely end the man's life, White Owl hauled him up to his feet. "You will stay here until we decide your fate."

While the brave used the strap of the man's own possibles satchel to tie him to a sturdy trunk, Hugh pushed himself to his feet and did a mental check for serious injury. Nothing broken. The bruises and burns would fade, and the pounding in his head would subside.

A glance at Louis showed his brother's body unmoved. Pain tried to crush Hugh's chest, but he couldn't give in to it yet. He had to find Watkuese and Pop-pank and make sure they were well, but he hated to take his focus from the two men lying on the ground until he knew they would no longer be a threat.

He did his best to build a barrier around his emotions as he scooped up a rifle from the ground and checked first one attacker, then the next. Neither man breathed.

Now to find his girls.

Turning slowly so his world didn't start spinning again, he looked to the place he'd last seen them, frozen at the end of a rifle barrel.

The pair stood in almost the same place. Watkuese looked as noble as the Nimiipuu princess she was, though something about her raised chin made him wonder how much pain lay beneath the surface. She clutched her daughter to her side, tucked a little behind.

Pop-pank gripped Watkuese's tunic as she peered around. Her eyes still loomed wide, but no longer with terror. Sadness weighed heavily in them. This was not a sight any child should see.

As if Watkuese heard his thoughts, she turned to her daughter and knelt in front of her, pulling Pop-pank's focus away from the awful scene.

Hugh could no longer avoid what he had to do. Stealing himself, he turned to face his brother's limp body.

He crouched and pressed fingers against his baby brother's neck, fighting the tears that burned hot just behind his eyes. Even though Louis hadn't moved throughout the fight, Hugh couldn't stop hoping he would feel lifeblood throb through his veins.

But...did it?

He adjusted his fingers and held his breath. *Yes*. A steady pulse thrummed there.

His own heart hammered as he dropped to his knees and carefully rolled his brother over to lie face up, bracing his head so it didn't flop. "Louis?"

No sign he'd been heard. What should he do? His brother's mouth was closed, but when Hugh placed a finger under his nose, a slight brush of air moved over his skin. Louis was definitely alive.

Joy surged through him. But he needed help. Maybe Watkuese would know how to wake Louis up without hurting him. He glanced around and found her kneeling over another body, Pop-pank standing a little behind her.

The man on the ground...White Owl.

He lay motionless, though he'd been fighting just moments before. What more had happened?

She looked up and met Hugh's gaze, her own eyes drawn with worry. She must've seen the question on his face, for she answered it. "He's unconscious. He's lost a lot of blood."

A knot of grief pressed in Hugh's chest. The brave had fought valiantly. Had maybe even saved Hugh's life. Surely she would be able to nurse him back to health.

Her gaze dropped to Louis, and fresh pain clouded her expression. "He is...?"

Hugh shook his head, then almost regretted the action when pain stabbed through him. "He lives. I can't get him to wake up though."

Hope lit her face. "Talk to him. Give him some water. A little splashed in his mouth and on his face."

Yes. He glanced toward the fire where a pot sat beside the coals. A small bit of liquid lay inside.

After pulling the pot over beside Louis, he used his hands to dribble a bit on his forehead. "Wake up, Louis. No sleeping late this time." The thought nearly choked him. What he wouldn't give for a thousand more mornings when he had to nudge his snoring brother out of the bedroll. He might even let Louis sleep late any time he wished if he survived this.

He *had* to survive.

CHAPTER 14

"Come on, Louis. Open your eyes." Hugh cupped his hands full of water and streamed it down his brother's cheeks. The fire had warmed the liquid so it didn't have quite the effect snow or ice might have.

Louis's eyes flicked open, and joy washed through him. *Thank You, God.*

Hugh sat back on his heels and watched as his brother blinked, slowly taking in first the sky, then Hugh's face. He seemed to struggle to focus.

"It's good to have you back." Far more than good.

Louis squinted. "What happened?"

"I was going to ask you." He flicked a glance to where Watkuese was still bent over White Owl. "I came from hunting to find three strangers here—Frenchmen. You were out cold. One of them had White Owl on the ground kicking him while another searched our packs. For whiskey, I think. The third held a gun on Watkuese and Pop-pank." His anger seeped back in as that image replayed in his mind.

"Poppy. Are the girls safe?" Louis started to turn his head but stopped with a wince.

Hugh glanced at them once more. "Don't seem to be hurt." At least not physically. Pop-pank was watching him and Louis with a sober expression. Maybe it would help her to see his brother alive and talking.

He motioned her over. "Louis's asking for you."

She stood and walked toward him obediently. Watkuese sent him a grateful look, then turned back to her ministrations with White Owl. She seemed to be wrapping something around his head. She might need help.

Pop-pank stopped a little distance from Louis, maybe afraid to get too close. Hugh patted the ground beside his brother. Perhaps these two could keep each other company while he went to Watkuese.

When Pop-pank sank down beside him, Louis gave her a tight smile. "Hello there, Poppy. You're just the girl to help me feel better."

Hugh rested a hand on her shoulder and gentled his voice. "I bet he'd like a drink of water. Can you scoop some for him with this cup?" He handed her the tin, then stood. "If you'll take care of Louis for me, I'll help with your uncle."

She gave a somber nod and dipped the cup in the pot of water. Hopefully, Louis could help bring back her smile.

Hugh turned his focus to the brave lying on the ground not far from the man tied to the tree. The Frenchman had slumped sideways, clearly in pain but still awake. Hugh moved around behind the trunk to make sure the scoundrel's hands were tied securely. White Owl had managed a tight knot before passing out. Good fellow.

As Hugh knelt beside him, opposite from Watkuese, she glanced up at him. A frown gathered on her brow. "He's lost much blood. A cut from when they struck him with the gun, I think. I've bandaged it, and the bleeding has finally slowed." She hesitated. He'd never seen her look so uncertain.

"What can I do to help?"

She glanced toward the fire, then at Louis and Pop-pank, then at the supplies and bedrolls. "We need to make him comfortable. A bed by the fire, I think, so he stays warm. I'll give him water and make a broth to help restore his blood."

Hugh pushed up to his feet. Those things he could do. "I'll lay out a fur by the fire, then move him onto it. I brought fresh meat for that stew." He needed to go for more water, too, but he hated to leave the camp. There were the deer and goat carcasses to retrieve also. Those weren't worth risking any of these lives for, but he hated to lose so much good meat, not when it might be sorely needed in a few days.

One task at a time.

After readying a fur pallet for White Owl, Hugh hoisted him up in both arms. He nearly doubled over with the strain of carrying him, but he was pretty sure Watkuese would object if he dragged the fellow across the ground or flopped him over his shoulder. Maybe she possessed more tender affection for this brave than he'd thought. Perhaps seeing him so injured had revealed her deep affections. If not, all the nursing care he'd need could bring it on.

Hugh couldn't think about that now. White Owl had fought valiantly and deserved everything they could do for him. And if Hugh really cared about Watkuese, he would want her to be happy. Even with another man.

He might have plunked the warrior down harder then he should have on the fur, but his straining muscles simply gave way. Watkuese didn't object, but White Owl did release a moan.

At least that meant he was alert enough to feel pain. A good thing, though he might not think so at that moment.

Pop-pank seemed to have settled in well with Louis, so this might be a good time for Hugh to get water. He had to make sure the group would be safe while he was gone, though. These three attackers might have a larger group waiting for them.

He wasn't willing to chance someone coming to look for

them. He knew exactly how desperate the craving for whiskey could make a man. He'd been backhanded to the floor more than once because he'd simply been in his father's way during a search.

Watkuese was adjusting a bandage around White Owl's head, but when Hugh touched her shoulder, her gaze jerked up to him. He motioned for her to follow him. He'd rather not let Pop-pank hear anything that would frighten her even more. The girl needed to feel safe.

He led Watkuese to the edge of camp, where they could speak without being heard. When he turned to face her, Watkuese stared up at him with worry playing in her gaze. "What is it?"

He hadn't meant to add to her concerns. He wanted to ease her fears, to make her feel safe. She deserved to know beyond doubt that he would protect her until his last breath. Saying it would mean little, and he sure hoped he wouldn't have to prove it. But he had to do something to help her feel his promise.

He meant only to cup his hands around her upper arms, but when he touched her, she came to him, pressing herself against his chest. His body responded, wrapping his arms around her, tucking her close. Closer.

Was she trembling? He pulled her tighter, resting his cheek on top of her head. Closing her in a protective shell. The burn of emotion in his throat was becoming too familiar. There was too much at stake loving people. Too much to lose. But he couldn't make himself stop. Not with his brother and not with this woman.

For long moments, he held her, letting her choose when she was ready to pull away. Though in truth, he'd rather she never left him.

At last, she eased back, and he loosened his hold, letting his hands slip away until he cupped her arms again. She stared up at him, and with her this close, it took everything in him not to lean in and taste her mouth once more.

But this was a time for comfort, not passion. Maybe the two went together sometimes, but if that was what she needed, he had no doubt Watkuese would show him. She'd initiated the kiss last time, after all.

For now, he leaned in and pressed his lips to her forehead. It seemed the right thing—the way to show he cared and that he would do whatever she needed of him.

Her eyes creased in a look that was both tender and thankful. She reached up and cupped his stubbled cheek. "You're a good man, Hugh Charpentier." The way she spoke his name in her lilting cadence made his hurt surge.

Then she straightened, which seemed to be a sign for him to drop his arms. "What did you wish to say?" She sent a quick glance toward the injured men and her daughter.

That's right. They had no time for long tender moments right now. "I'm going to get water. I'll leave my rifle with you. Have you ever shot a gun?"

She nodded, though her expression looked hesitant. "A few times."

He quickly reloaded the weapon and walked through the steps to fire it, then watched as she mimicked him. She may not be a sharpshooter, but she might only need to point the rifle to accomplish what she needed to.

Hopefully she wouldn't even have to do that.

After gathering the pot and all their canteens, he ran toward the spring, ignoring the pounding in his head. If only it wasn't so far from camp. Why hadn't they searched for water before choosing a place the night before?

When he finally returned to the group, Watkuese was seated beside White Owl with the rifle in her lap. He should have alerted her that it was him approaching. He might have been met with a bullet through his chest.

But she must have realized it was him, for she only met him with a nod. When he set the water pot by Watkuese, she scooped a cup full immediately. "Thank you." But her focus remained on White Owl as she dribbled some in his mouth.

Hugh crouched beside his brother again. "You look better now." More alert, though he still lay flat.

Louis patted Pop-pank's knee. "Our girl here knows just how to cheer a fellow."

Pop-pank gave a shy smile, and the sweetness of the look made Hugh want to do the same. Louis sure had the touch that could brighten even the worst situation.

But as Hugh glanced up and his gaze took in the injured man tied to the tree, the weight settled back in his chest.

He had two bodies to bury. And a living man he must decide what to do with. The last thing he wanted was to turn the stranger loose, but the only other option he could stomach was to bring him along. Would that put the girls in more danger?

He had to make the right decision here. Their lives were at stake.

CHAPTER 15

*W*atkuese's hands still trembled when she let herself remember the attack. Especially now in the final moments of night before morning slipped in. Hearing Louis's cry of pain. Spinning to see him crumble to the ground beneath the black-bearded one.

White Owl had jumped into action, tomahawk raised as he charged the stranger. But two others appeared from nowhere, and the attack of all three sent him to the ground too.

Oh, White Owl. Between the blow to his head and the knife wound she'd found on his leg, his lifeblood had nearly left him. He still lived, though, and she would do everything she could to help his body rebuild what he'd lost.

She glanced toward where he slept. She could just make out the shadow of his bedding in the darkness. Perhaps she should rise and offer him more broth. The livers she'd stewed would help restore him. But maybe it would be just as well to wait for more daylight.

She tightened her arm around Pop-pank. In those moments when she'd stared into the dark muzzle of the gun, all she'd thought about was how hard it would be for Pop-pank to lose one more person important to her. Maybe the girl couldn't yet show that Watkuese mattered, but in her heart, Watkuese knew she did. They were connected, maybe not yet as mother and daughter, but need wove them together in an impenetrable fabric. Watkuese couldn't let the girl endure another loss so soon.

She glanced at the sky once more. Light had begun to soften the eastern horizon, which meant she should rise. Hugh had done so much last evening, surely he wouldn't get up to prepare morning food. She should have it ready when he first woke. He'd already replenished their water supply again just before bedding down. He'd also brought in the game he'd brought down during his hunt. She would need to care for the meat and hides today.

When she slipped out of her furs and stood, her ankle ached as usual. She shouldn't need the walking stick this morning though. Maybe she wouldn't need it at all today, since they wouldn't be riding.

Her gaze slipped over the two injured men. How long before they would be ready to travel again? The blow to Louis's head had been a hard one, and he still couldn't remember much from yesterday, but she suspected he would be up and moving around by noon. Perhaps ready to travel by the morrow.

White Owl? It might be a few more days for him.

After she slipped into the trees to take care of morning needs, she stepped back into camp and knelt to stoke the fire. The flames sprang to life quickly, for she'd added wood in the night when she rose to feed White Owl more broth.

She glanced up, and her gaze snagged on the tree where the remaining attacker was tied. How had she forgotten about him? She strained to see through the dim morning light.

Had he slipped down to the base of the trunk for better sleep? The grass there lay flat with no lump that could be a man.

Fear sizzled through her, rising in bumps along her arms. Had he gotten loose?

She pushed to her feet and hobbled two steps toward the tree. Maybe he'd worked himself around to the other side for some reason.

But no. The man was gone.

She backed away from the spot, scanning the darkness in every direction. No one.

She had to wake Hugh. Maybe he'd moved the stranger in the night for some reason. Turning toward the sleeping forms, her ankle barely ached as she scrambled to Hugh's side. She touched his shoulder and kept her voice quiet. "Hugh." Once more she turned to the darkness around camp. Was the man out there watching?

Hugh jerked up to a sitting position. "What is it?" He vaulted to his feet, pulling out his knife as he moved a little in front of her, peering out into the night.

She let herself breathe a little easier. He would protect them. He had both the skills and the desire to do so. "The man who was tied...did you move him?"

Hugh's head whipped toward the tree, and he took a step toward it. "Where did...?" He paused, and once more he scanned the darkness around them, this time with a great deal more intention. Even as he searched, he spoke to her. "Get the rifle I gave you. Have it ready just in case."

He reached down for his own gun, tucking his knife back in its sheath. He still carried the weapon he'd taken from one of the dead men, leaving his own rifle with her. She knew too little of the weapons to know the difference. Maybe he was allowing her to keep the one he'd already taught her to use. But she should offer to switch later in case the weapon meant something to him.

She held her rifle at the ready as Hugh approached the tree. He stared at the ground where the attacker had sat, circled the trunk, then moved into the woods. Maybe he'd found the escaping tracks. Hugh had proven himself an expert tracker.

When he disappeared into the shadows, the camp felt emptier than a moment before. She glanced around again. Did she sense someone watching, or was that her imagination?

When her focus slipped down to the sleeping figures in her charge, White Owl's eyes were open. He was the one she'd felt watching, though the rest of him hadn't moved.

She kept the rifle at the ready as she limped over to him. "How are you feeling?" He hadn't seemed this aware since before his collapse.

"Stronger." His gaze shifted from her to the darkness outside the camp. "The white man has gone to find the one who escaped?"

"Yes." She searched the place where Hugh had disappeared. "Hugh is an excellent tracker. He'll find him if it's possible."

She could feel White Owl's gaze shifting to her, but she didn't meet his look, just kept her own focus on any shadows shifting among the trees. She wasn't ready to admit what might be growing between her and Hugh. In truth, she still wasn't sure exactly what it was. She only knew that she respected him and was drawn to him in a way she'd never felt for another.

And he made her feel safe. When she'd been cocooned in his arms yesterday like a papoose in a cradle board, she'd felt as if she'd finally found the place she belonged.

She swallowed, doing her best to push away those thoughts. For now, she had to focus on watching, being ready for wherever threat arose.

At last, a voice drifted from the shadows among the trees. "It's Hugh."

The tension in her body eased, but she didn't lower the gun until he appeared, striding through the trunks. As much as she wanted to go to him, she waited for him to approach. White Owl would want to hear his report too.

Hugh nodded to the brave. "Good to see you awake." He turned and made a full circle, peering into the much lighter shadows around the camp again. "I tracked him to the spring where we've been getting water. He must have walked in the creek down the mountain to where it feeds into a larger stream. I could spend the day searching both directions of that water to find which way he went, but I'd rather not be gone from here so long. Since he was traveling away from us, there's a chance he won't be back."

And a chance he would. The unspoken words hovered in the air. Had the stranger gone to gather up more companions and return for another attack? Hopefully he now knew they had no strong drink, but revenge might be an even stronger motive to return.

"We'll have to stand guard." Hugh turned to White Owl. "I'll handle it until you and Louis feel well enough to sit up with a rifle."

"I can do that now." The words came in Louis's sleepy tone, and he pushed the covers off him. As he sat, the shadows hid his pain, but one of his hands reached up to hold his head.

Watkuese moved to the pot of water to scoop him a drink. When she brought him the cup, he accepted it with a quiet, "Thank you."

While he drank, she placed her hand on top of his head. "I'm going to feel the bump, but I'll be gentle."

His body tensed under her fingers as she slid them down toward the knot near the base of his skull. He flinched before she reached the spot. The lump didn't seem to have gone down any. Too bad there wasn't snow to pack around the area. It wouldn't be an easy thing to soak his head in a pot of water. Perhaps he could lie in the spring for a while.

By the time Watkuese had fed broth to White Owl and cooked some of the deer meat from Hugh's hunt yesterday, Poppank sat up on their sleeping mat. The girl had slept late, and her mussed hair attested to how restless she'd been in the night. The bad dream had returned—or perhaps this was a new one—but Watkuese had realized the signs early and awakened the girl. The song Pop-pank's mother had always hummed while they picked berries usually cleared the nightmare away and allowed the child to drift into peaceful sleep.

Hugh had crouched by the packs, sorting through the damage from the day before, but he paused to smile at Pop-pank. "Good morning. Did you sleep well?"

She nodded, still wearing that sleepy gaze. Then she held her hands out to him in the way every child asks to be picked up. She wanted Hugh to carry her?

He seemed as surprised as Watkuese, and he even flicked a glance her way with a question in his gaze. She nodded, just in case he thought he needed permission. Pop-pank rarely showed a connection with others, so this step of trust with Hugh felt significant.

He stood and closed the distance between them, then scooped up the girl and let her sit on his arm. With his free hand, he brushed the silky black strands of hair out of her face. "Are you hungry? I smell fresh deer meat, and it's making my belly rumble." He patted his flat middle and won a shy smile from Pop-pank.

With both arms around her now, he ambled forward. "I need to check on the horses too. Maybe after we eat, I'll bring them into camp and you can help me rub them down. They deserve a bit of attention after carrying us so far these past few days."

Watkuese couldn't take her eyes off the pair, the big strong man and her petite little girl. He was so gentle with her, and Pop-pank soaked in his attention like a parched child drinking water. Watkuese's heart ached with the beauty of the scene. She could almost forget the remnants of fear from the stranger who might be lurking outside their camp. And her worry for White Owl.

A glance at the brave showed his eyes were closed. His breathing didn't seem deep enough for him to be asleep. Was he trying to block out the sight of Hugh with his niece, or merely succumbing to his exhaustion?

Either way, she needed to be careful not to raise his ire, especially where Pop-pank was concerned. He was the only blood relative the girl had left. That detail mattered, and Watkuese should keep the thought in mind.

Perhaps she should have considered it more before refusing his request to marry. If he asked her again, should her answer change? What would truly be best for this child who'd stolen her heart?

She'd already promised herself she would give her life to protect Pop-pank. Should she give her freedom as well?

CHAPTER 16

"When Louis was a boy just a little younger than you, he was always climbing things." Hugh leaned against the rock above the spring as he watched Pop-pank scramble from one stone to the next to reach the top of the cluster. "The problem was, he liked to climb up, but he didn't like to climb down."

Pop-pank paused on the top rock and peered back the way she'd come. "How did he get down?"

Her wide eyes made it too hard to resist a smile. "Sometimes he would come down backwards, the same way he went up. And sometimes I had to climb up and get him."

She looked at Hugh, then Watkuese, who sat with her ankle soaking in the cold water. In an expression so much like her adoptive mother, Pop-pank lifted her chin. "I can climb down."

She eyed the boulders again as if she planned to go headfirst. Thankfully, that idea didn't stick, and she turned around to lower her feet from one rock to the next.

Hugh stood close enough that he could leap forward and catch her if she started to tumble, but the girl maneuvered the pile well and finally jumped to the ground beside him.

She looked like she might start back up the rocks, so he motioned toward the tiny stream. "I think I saw something sparkle in the water. It might be a loose stone you can take back with you."

While Pop-pank peeled off her moccasins, Hugh checked their surroundings again, straining for any sound or sight that seemed off. They'd not seen any sign of the attacker who'd escaped two nights before, but he couldn't let his guard down.

He'd managed to keep Pop-pank in the camp all day yesterday, but by late morning today, her pent-up energy was almost impossible to contain. A walk to the spring for her to play while her mother soaked her ankle seemed the best idea, and he'd come along as guard.

Louis was up and moving around camp—albeit slowly—so he could keep guard there. Even White Owl had been sitting up with a rifle in his lap when they left. The man had only stood a few times, just long enough to stagger to a tree to relieve himself.

How long did it take for one to regain strength from a blood loss like his? Another couple days at least, Hugh would guess. He had a feeling White Owl would suggest they push on as soon as he thought he could stay upright in the saddle. The man was tough—he'd proven that.

"You're good with her." Watkuese's voice murmured just loud enough to reach his ears. She kept her gaze on her daughter, who had waded a short way down the slope. One of her hands contained the stones she'd picked up so far. She would likely need to use her skirt to carry them all at the rate she was finding rocks she liked.

"I'm glad she seems like herself again. I was worried after she stayed so quiet that first day."

Watkuese nodded, but a frown etched lines in her brow. He shouldn't have reminded her of the attack. Shouldn't have made her worry about the girl. Now he had to think of something that would ease that concern.

"She reminds me some of Louis when he was that age. They work through an upset so quickly." Was that the right thing to say?

She glanced up and studied him for a moment. "I suspect you helped a lot with his raising. That must be why you have an easy way with Pop-pank."

He swallowed. She hadn't asked a direct question, so he didn't have to answer. But part of him wanted her to know that side of his past. "I was there when my ma died. When Louis was born. Our pa was drunk. I don't think he even knew she was dying. She asked me to take care of Louis. To see that he was safe and grew up to be a good man."

His mouth had gone dry, so he swallowed again to bring back moisture. "When she was...gone...Louis wouldn't stop crying. I knew he had to eat and we didn't have a milk cow, so I took him to our neighbor who'd just had a baby girl. They agreed to take Louis in and let me stay on to work for them so I could be with him."

The dark pools of her eyes watched him with a tenderness that kept him from wanting to pull back. Kept him from resurrecting his defenses after sharing something so...well, he'd never told anyone what Ma had said.

When she spoke, her voice was gentle. "Your mother would be proud of you. I suspect she never imagined how well you would carry out her wishes."

He wanted to drown in her approval, but he couldn't. Not when he didn't deserve it. "I should have made Raphael come with us—our middle brother, exactly halfway between mine and Louis's ages. He admired Pa so much. Why, I never understood. I guess he just craved his attention. He wouldn't leave Pa, though I told him he had to. With Louis bawling and half starved, I couldn't wait any longer, and my arms were too full to drag Rafael. Later, it seemed like, if he wanted to be with Pa so much, I should let him." He cleared the ache from his voice. "I wish I hadn't. I wish I'd pushed until he was away from our father's influence."

"He was Colette's first husband?" Watkuese's voice stayed soft.

He nodded. "I think he really did try to be good to her. But when he would drink..." That last time, Raphael had gone too far. Louis had seen it happen from a distance, had seen Rafael strike out at Colette. She grabbed the nearest tool she could reach to protect herself and her unborn babe. The blow had killed their brother, and as much as Hugh mourned him, he didn't blame Colette.

He blamed himself for not making Rafael come to the Heinrichs' all those years ago. And he blamed himself for not coming around often enough when Rafael was grown, for not seeing how much he'd begun to be like their father.

He and Rafael were both too much like Pa—in looks, in mannerisms, in personality. Hugh'd had the benefit of living at the Heinrichs' for those six years, but he'd spent the first ten years of his life under his father's rule. He would always be just as prone to fall into those temptations as Pa and Raphael had been. It was in their blood, even Pa had said so.

Which was why he could never subject a woman—not any woman, but especially not Watkuese—to what he could become.

~

*H*ugh watched Watkuese dip a cup in the pot of special broth she'd made for White Owl. Pop-pank lay on her sleeping mat, her steady breaths showing she'd finally succumbed to an afternoon nap. She'd wanted to go with Louis to move the horses to new grazing, but Watkuese had seen the girl's exhaustion in the shadows under her eyes.

Hugh sat a little away from Watkuese and White Owl, rifle across his lap so he would be ready for anything. As she handed the cup of broth to the brave, she gave him a smile that twisted the knife of jealousy in Hugh's belly.

He'd kept his distance since they walked to the spring the day before, as distant as he could when they were all nearly confined to this camp. He willed his heart not to long for her, not to crave her look, not to hope for that very smile she'd just given to White Owl. But he simply wasn't strong enough to stop this yearning that had grown so intense within him.

She adjusted the bandage around White Owl's head, and Hugh tried to look away. Tried to school his expression and pretend he wasn't affected. That he didn't care.

What he felt inside was so much more than care.

When Watkuese turned from the brave to shift the pots beside the fire, White Owl spoke in a tone loud enough for Hugh to hear. "When the sun rises, we will ride again."

Watkuese jerked her gaze up to study the brave, and it wasn't hard to read her thoughts. As Hugh had come to expect from her, she paused long enough to think through what she was about to do, then voiced her opinion. "Should we wait one more day? We have a good camp here. There is no reason to hurry."

White Owl glanced around as though checking the accuracy of her words. "It is a good camp, but I'm ready." His gaze landed on Pop-pank, then moved to Watkuese. "It's time for you both to be home."

Home. These last few days, Hugh hadn't let himself linger too long on that word and what it meant. And he sure didn't allow his mind to go there now.

But the word, combined with the three people before him, made him feel so much like the outsider. The dark hue of their skin matched, as did the rich black of their hair. His own murky brown didn't even match Louis's, with his blonde curls just like their mother's.

Hugh studied the trees around them for any sign of the attacker who'd escaped, not just to avoid watching the little family forming before his eyes.

"I don't think you're ready to ride up and down these mountains. Another day will give you more strength." Only Watkuese would argue with a Shoshone warrior in his prime and tell him he wasn't strong enough.

"Creator Father will give me strength. As He did during the battle."

Hugh turned back to see the man's expression. Was he speaking of the sun or some of the lesser gods the Shoshone worshiped? White Owl's face revealed nothing, though he was looking at Watkuese as though expecting her to comment on his words.

And she did. "Who is this Creator Father you speak of?"

White Owl glanced at Hugh, then returned his focus to Watkuese. "He is the One the white men know. Two missionaries came to our village while you were gone and told us more of Creator Father. I was not quick to believe what they said, but I have seen His power since then and know He is real. He uses His strength for good, as when He renewed me to finish the battle here." He motioned toward the place where the bushy bearded man had stood over him. "He will give me that same strength until we are back with our people."

Hugh couldn't stop himself from studying the man. White Owl had become a Christian? That wasn't a title even Hugh claimed. He knew of God, certainly, but he also knew enough to realize a true Christian actually *liked* God.

One more reason White Owl was the better match for Watkuese. He would tell her about the Almighty, and perhaps she would follow Him as well. Hugh should tell Watkuese this Shoshone brave was the better man for her. As soon as they reached the village, before he and Louis left, he would make himself tell her to marry Pop-pank's uncle.

Watkuese again stirred the broth while she studied White Owl. The pause was much longer this time, and the weight of her silence seemed to thicken the air. "I am—"

The sound of footsteps through the trees stopped her words, and Hugh surged to his feet, lifting his rifle so it would be ready to aim. The steps were loud, as though someone was running. Probably Louis returning from the horses, but why move so fast?

"It's me." Louis's voice called from the shadows of the trunks just as Hugh made out his form. His brother slowed to a walk as he entered camp, his shoulders heaving as he drew in deep breaths. He stopped in the open area between Hugh and the others.

"What is it?" Impatience pressed through Hugh. If there was a threat, he needed to know how to face it.

Louis swallowed, still breathing hard. "I was moving the horses around the side of the mountain, farther away where there's a patch of grass that should last them a couple days. Just before we got there, I heard a rock falling from higher up the mountain. Not a boulder, but big enough for me to hear the sound pretty well."

His brother paused to suck in a deep breath, and Hugh had to clamp his jaw to keep from telling him to cut the story short. Louis always could spin a yarn, but this wasn't the time for a drawn out tale.

"Anyway, when I looked up, I saw someone running."

Hugh's insides tightened even more. "Where did he go? Was he the man who escaped? Did you go after him?"

Louis shot him a look. "I only saw a flash of him. He was jumping behind some boulders. I went after him, but when I got to those rocks, he was gone. I had no idea where, so I came back here to report." Louis straightened and gave a stiff Army salute. "That's all I know, captain, sir." Only Louis could send him such a cheeky grin at a moment like this.

Hugh would have popped him in the jaw in their younger days, but he refrained now. "Was he the attacker who escaped?"

His brother shrugged. "I couldn't see his face. He wore dark brown leggings, almost black. I think he had a vest on over a fabric shirt, maybe a buckskin vest. No hat."

That sure sounded like the man. The leggings weren't black, just a very, very soiled brown.

Hugh scanned the edges of the camp once more, then faced the three watching him. "White Owl's right. We should start out tomorrow morning." He turned and aimed his next words at Watkuese, but he didn't let himself meet her gaze. "You two need to go home where you'll be safe."

CHAPTER 17

*T*he tension that had pressed so thick around them was finally easing now that they'd ridden nearly two days from the place of the attack. It didn't surprise her that Hugh and White Owl stayed on constant alert, rifles in hand no matter what they were doing.

It *did* surprise her that Louis did almost the same. His easy-going demeanor had tightened into a keen alertness. She'd sometimes wondered if his relaxed nature came from a bit of laziness or from a deeper ability to soften tense moments and brighten the days of those around him.

Now, she had no doubt he possessed a unique insight. A sharper intelligence than most people might credit him for.

As much as she appreciated the way they were all three working so hard to guard her and Pop-pank, she couldn't help looking forward to being in her quiet lodge in the village where she could forget about being constantly on guard.

Pop-pank had wrapped her arms around Watkuese's waist, and Watkuese pressed a hand over hers. Her daughter had acted a little disappointed when Watkuese asked her to move from Louis's saddle to her own. But at least she didn't sulk. Having

Pop-pank where Watkuese could touch her and know she was safe eased the tightness in her chest.

One more day.

According to White Owl, by the time the sun set on the morrow, they should reach the village. The band had moved to their winter camp while she and Pop-pank were gone, so he knew their location better than she did—one of the few good things about him coming after them.

She shouldn't think that, though. If he hadn't been there when those three men attacked, they might all be gone now.

But gone where? She still couldn't believe White Owl had accepted the white man's God. He usually distrusted anything the white men did or said. For him to say their God was real and to follow the Creator Father, as he called Him...well, she still couldn't quite make sense of it.

Last night, she'd asked him more about what the missionaries had said, and he'd spoken of two places that people might go when they died—heaven or hell. Those who followed Creator Father would go to a wonderful place called heaven and live with Him there, never ever dying. Those who didn't follow Him would go to hell, where fire would always burn them but never burn them up. The misery would last forever.

As awful as that sounded, she'd never been one to make a choice because of a threat. She needed to know more before she decided whether she would follow the white man's God. How had White Owl chosen so easily?

And Hugh... Why had he never spoken of his God? He was a white man, so surely he followed Creator Father. Didn't he?

She glanced back at the man who now rode double with Louis. Hugh still dismounted and walked often, but the last two days he'd taken to riding with his brother on the level areas that would be easiest for the horse.

Hugh nodded to acknowledge her look but didn't offer a smile. There had been a distance between them these last few days. She couldn't quite say when it had started—maybe after they'd gone to the spring—and she had no idea why.

Surely *she* wasn't doing something to place a barrier between them. Did he think she felt an attraction to White Owl? After the tender moments she'd shared with Hugh, could he really think that?

Ahead of her, White Owl slowed his horse enough to draw her attention. In the distance, another figure approached. Two of them, horses with riders.

Hugh must have seen them too, for he pushed his mount around her to ride up beside White Owl. The two horses formed a sort of shield in front of her and Pop-pank, and she was grateful.

"Who is that?" Pop-pank's arms tightened around her as she leaned around Watkuese's arm just enough to see.

"I don't know." The figures were still too far away to tell which tribe they belonged to. Pop-pank had spoken loudly enough for Watkuese to hear, but there was a chance White Owl might have as well. Would he answer when he knew? Or was he the kind of man who deemed women not worth wasting time on?

His brother hadn't felt that way. He'd treated Kimana like an equal. No...more than that. He'd treated her like she mattered more than he did.

And Kimana had done the same with him. The love between them had been clear not just in the words they said, which was unusual enough with the Shoshone. But it showed even more in their actions. A tender look. A gentle touch. An encouraging smile.

Watkuese wanted that. If she ever agreed to marry a man, she would not settle for anything less than the love Kimana had shared with her husband.

"They are Shoshone, but not from our village." White Owl's quiet voice tugged her back from the ache of her thoughts.

She couldn't let her mind wander like that when strangers approached. Nor should she let her thoughts linger on the topic of love at all. It would only bring pain. Especially since she'd begun to think a love like that might be possible with Hugh.

He was certainly a man she could respect, and her heart had connected with him. But if he didn't feel the same, as his actions these past few days made it seem, she would do best to tighten her defenses.

"Do you know them?" Tension hummed in Hugh's voice as he spoke to White Owl.

Watkuese leaned to get a better look at the approaching strangers. Neither of the men looked familiar to her, but she'd never strayed far from the village while she lived with the Shoshone. White Owl might have seen them on a hunting trip.

"I have met the one in front. He is mild, someone we do not need to fear."

She inhaled a deep breath then released it, trying to soothe the knot in her middle. This would be a simple meeting on the trail then. Perhaps they would hear news of what had been happening while she and Pop-pank were gone. White Owl had only told her about the people in their village, not the other bands in the area.

They halted their horses when the newcomers reached them, and she could easily see the curiosity on both men's faces as they looked from Hugh and Louis riding double on Snowy, to White Owl, to her and Pop-pank tucked behind.

White Owl led the conversation, as she'd expected. "It is good we meet, my friend. You have come from the grassland?"

The man shook his head. "From your village. We had business to discuss with your Chief Twin Elk and are now returning to our families."

From her village? Watkuese held herself still so she didn't miss a word of news.

"Twin Elk said you have gone to bring back your woman

and the daughter of your brother." The man nodded toward Watkuese.

Much as she tried not to, her body stiffened. She was not White Owl's woman, but this was not the time to quibble. She would only draw attention she didn't want if she spoke up.

White Owl nodded. "As you see." He didn't say anything about Hugh and Louis, but the look the man sent them showed how much he wanted to ask. He would likely skirt around the question for a while.

The newcomer motioned to the trail. "This way you travel, you are going to the old camp?"

She couldn't see White Owl's face to know if the question confused him as much as it did her. This was the season the village would have settled in at the winter camp.

"Our people have moved again?" No confusion sounded in his voice, and though it was a question, his tone rang with calm assurance.

The corners of the man's mouth tipped as he nodded. "The water was not good at the winter camp, so they have moved north to another valley your chief knows of."

"Where is this valley?"

Something in this fellow's expression didn't settle right in Watkuese's middle. He liked having news White Owl didn't know, that was clear. But did the narrowing of his eyes mean something more?

He pointed to the north. "Between two peaks that rise higher than those around them. The valley is wide with a river running through."

She nearly snorted. That could describe almost every valley from here northward.

But White Owl must have decided it wasn't worth questioning this man further. He nodded. "I am glad we meet, my friend." After making the sign of friendship, he reined his horse around the two men.

Hugh did the same, and with his hand, made a low gesture for her to come alongside him. The strangers wouldn't have been able to see it, and when she nudged her mount forward, she was tucked in between White Owl and Hugh and Louis.

Protected.

She didn't spare the strangers a glance as they passed. But that didn't stop her from worrying about what they hadn't said.

And the truth of what they had.

~

White Owl clearly didn't like the meeting with his friend any more than Hugh did.

Once they passed out of sight, the man kept riding instead of pausing to discuss what was said. And he didn't alter their direction to the north toward this new camp.

White Owl must be worried the two braves had turned to follow them.

They rode another quarter hour perhaps before White Owl motioned to a cluster of trees. "We can rest the horses here."

As soon as they dismounted, Hugh turned to the man, waiting for him to share his thoughts.

The Shoshone brave stared down the trail the way they'd come. "It is possible he spoke the truth. I heard talk of problems with the water before I left. Twin Elk would have moved quickly so the new camp could be set before the first snow. I'm not certain where the new valley is, but I can think of two places within a day's ride." He turned to Hugh and met his gaze. "It would be wise for one of us to ride ahead and find the village before all go."

A rock weighted Hugh's gut. White Owl must mean for Hugh to go, and that made sense. He was the strongest, the healthiest. "I can find the camp." But part of him hated the thought of riding away from Watkuese and Pop-pank, of leaving their protection to others.

And leaving her with the brave who still seemed determined to win her. He needed to get used to that though, if he planned to tell Watkuese she should marry the man.

White Owl shook his head. "I know where to look. You are stronger, better able to protect."

For a long moment, the man held his gaze. It wasn't easy for him to leave the girls with Hugh, but he was doing what he felt best for them. That deserved respect, and Hugh would willingly give it.

He nodded his acceptance of the responsibility. "We'll wait until you return."

White Owl turned away, almost as though he couldn't face the thought any longer. He mounted his horse in a swift motion, the sign for the rest of them to do the same.

They didn't travel much farther before the brave again reined his horse in. He motioned to a spot tucked in the crook of a boulder and trees. "This is a good camp."

Hugh took in the ashes from previous fires. It appeared they'd reached a part of the trail more heavily traveled. This must be a regular overnight spot.

He peered through the trees but could see only rocky grass-land beyond. "There is water here?"

White Owl pointed to the boulder. "A spring beyond that rock." Instead of dismounting, he turned his horse so he faced them all. "I'll ride on. When I find the village, I'll come back to this place."

"You're riding tonight?" Watkuese's horse edged forward. "Sleep first, then you can leave in the morning."

When the brave looked at her, the hard set of his jaw eased, and the gentleness in his eyes became hard to witness. But Hugh didn't let himself turn away.

Even White Owl's voice softened when he spoke. "I'm strong

enough for now. I'll sleep when I need to. Stay here. Don't leave this place." His look turned pointed, as though he had experience with the way Watkuese's impulsiveness sometimes made her slip away quietly when she was determined to leave a place.

Watkuese nodded. After a final glance around, the Shoshone warrior turned his horse and trotted away.

CHAPTER 18

*A*fter White Owl disappeared around a bend in the trail, Hugh stepped to his gelding's side. Time they get settled in camp. He couldn't quite stand the way Watkuese stared after the brave, like she was pining for him already.

He tapped Pop-pank's knee where she sat behind her mother. "Are you ready to stretch your legs?"

The girl reached for him as she'd begun to do every time he helped her down from the horse. He took her in his arms and gave her a half spin before setting her on the ground. The smile that always flashed when he did that made him want to keep going, letting her fly around in circles until she giggled uncontrollably. Maybe one of these times he would.

For now, he and Louis settled the horses, unpacked supplies, and gathered wood, while Watkuese nursed a fire. White Owl's absence had hovered over them at first, but by the time Hugh finished his first bowl of meat stew, the evening felt just like one of their earlier days.

The difference was that he knew Watkuese better now. She and Pop-pank had burrowed a lasting place in his heart. When this journey ended, he would move on as he'd promised himself.

But he would be back to check on them, to bring Pop-pank what treasures he could find and make sure they both had everything they needed. Would she still have the horse doll he'd been making for her?

With White Owl.

The thought burned as he swallowed it down. He couldn't look at Watkuese. Somehow he had to kill this desire for her. If only it *were* merely desire—a physical longing. But every part of him had fallen for her, including his heart, and it would take years to stop loving her, if he ever managed at all.

Perhaps this was good for him. He'd determined never to marry, never to inflict himself and who he could become on any family. If he left his heart behind with Watkuese, there'd be no chance he'd fall for another woman who might threaten that promise.

The thought brought no comfort, but he could live with it. As long as he didn't let his gaze drift to Watkuese.

Even now, his eyes refused to obey, slipping over to her for quick glances as she refilled Pop-pank's bowl, then reached for his. "You would like more?"

He nodded, handing her the tin dish. Much more, and not just the stew.

Hugh hadn't even realized the silence that sank over them until Louis broke it by slapping his knees. "Watkuese, your food is always good. Thank you. Pop-pank, I saw rabbit tracks by the spring. Shall we follow the water and see what other animals we find?"

"Like beavers?" Pop-pank jumped to her feet, eagerness lighting her face. Louis reached out and tickled her belly. She giggled and danced out of his reach, then took off as he leaped up and gave chase.

"We might even see a bear—*roar*—who wants to eat you." Louis gave all the sound effects of an angry grizzly as Pop-pank's laughter rang through the dusky air. As the two disappeared through the trees, their chuckles and banter drifted back to camp.

Seeing Pop-pank so happy, just like a six-year-old girl should be, spread pleasure through Hugh like a warm blanket on a cold night. He looked back at Watkuese, whose own smile made her look like a dark-haired angel.

She met his gaze, and her grin turned a little shy. "You're both so good with her. I didn't know how I would help her learn to laugh again."

A burn clogged his throat even as the sound of laughter through the trees made him smile again. "Louis has that touch." He swallowed, trying to force down the knot. "And I'm glad. She's special."

Watkuese nodded, then dropped her focus to the pot still positioned near the coals. Her shyness seemed to grow, tying her tongue and building a barrier between them.

She began gathering the supplies she'd used in cooking, preparing for cleanup. He reached for the bowls they'd eaten from and stacked them. What could he say to break the silence? Even if he couldn't have her love, he couldn't stand the thought of losing Watkuese's friendship. What question could be benign enough to start a conversation?

Maybe the topic of food. "Do you...have supplies stored away for the winter? Who hunts for you?" As the word slipped out, he realized White Owl would likely be the one bringing her meat through these winter months. And she would prepare it for him to eat...as his wife.

"I have trade goods. I can barter for enough to feed us this winter. I'm usually able to harvest roots and berries to carry me until spring. And I work for a share of the buffalo hunts." She kept her focus on her task as she spoke, and he wanted desperately to reach over and lift her chin. To raise her gaze so he could see those dark pools that felt like home. To lose himself in them.

But he couldn't. Did she know why he couldn't? She knew he planned to take her to the village then leave, he'd said that at the beginning.

But maybe now she thought he'd changed his mind. Maybe since their kiss... Perhaps that was why she was acting so shy around him. Especially if tender feelings were growing between her and White Owl. Sometimes it seemed... Well he wasn't very good at deciphering a woman's thoughts, especially when her heart was involved.

He'd planned to wait until he said goodbye at the village to tell her she should marry White Owl. But perhaps he should say it now.

He looked at her once more, allowing himself only a heart-beat to appreciate her beauty, the way the firelight flickered off her dark skin. "Watkuese."

She jerked her face up, her intense eyes piercing him with a gaze that made his heart race. The awareness between them sparked stronger than the fire. No matter how much he told himself he would be leaving her soon—maybe even in a couple days—he couldn't fight the attraction, the way she pulled him in.

Maybe if she wasn't sitting so close. But she was. And he leaned in.

And she met him there.

Her mouth was no longer unschooled, yet still so tender and innocent. He savored every moment, every touch. Every taste of her richness. When he'd first met this woman, he hadn't imagined she would bring him to life like this.

But she did, and for this one kiss, he let himself truly live.

He had no idea how long the connection lasted, but he knew it was up to him to pull back. She trusted him, and he would guard her from anything that might bring pain. Especially himself.

He drew back just enough to rest his forehead on hers, his hands cradling her cheeks, cherishing the feel of her. He would take the memory of these moments with him forever, and he wanted to feel everything.

Watkuese pulled away first, far enough for their gazes to meet. He took in her beauty, stroked his thumb across the line of her jaw. Lost himself in those eyes a little longer. "You are the most remarkable woman I've ever met. Don't ever forget that."

Her eyes seemed to struggle with something—the question she couldn't decide whether she would ask or not.

Don't ask. He couldn't tell her goodbye tonight. Not yet. Couldn't speak of White Owl and all the reasons she should marry the man.

So instead, he pushed away from her. Stood. And walked into dusky shadows.

That's where Louis found him a half hour later.

His brother strolled toward him, a piece of buckskin rope twirling in one hand. Hugh sat on a fallen log next to a wide tree that offered ample back rest. Almost as comfortable as the settee the Heinrichs used to have. Not that Hugh had spent much time on the good furniture.

Louis settled on the edge of the log beside him. Hugh didn't move down to share his back rest. Though Louis was trying to make his manner seem casual, something in the air felt very intentional.

He didn't wait long before starting in. "So...it looks like you and Watkuese are getting along much better these days."

Before Hugh could remind himself not to react, his gaze shot to Louis. Had he seen...?

Louis's grin made the answer all too clear. Bright twinkles lit both eyes, and white teeth flashed. "She's quite a catch. You planning to marry her?"

A pinch tightened Hugh's chest, and he turned back to the patch of grass he'd been staring at for a quarter hour now. "I'm not the marrying kind."

A scoff came from Louis's direction. "Of course you are. You were made for it."

Hugh shook his head. Why did his brother always push so hard? He lifted his gaze toward the night sky, a few stars glittering between the clouds. "I'm too much like Pa. I wouldn't do that to any woman."

Louis didn't answer right away, and it made Hugh want to turn and see what he was thinking. But then his brother finally spoke. "You're not like Pa, Hugh. Not in the ways that matter. You're just like Ma."

Hugh looked at him, his throat aching as the image of their mother slipped through his mind. Even after all these years, he missed her. His voice rasped when he spoke again. "I wish you could have known her. She was good. And beautiful. Always kind, always a gentle word, always protected us. Whenever things got loud and scary, *she* was safe."

Louis met his gaze, his eyes glistening in the moonlight. "And that's you." Then he grimaced. "All except the beautiful part."

Then his focus grew earnest again. "You were Ma to me, Hugh. As wonderful as the Heinrichs were, you were my safe place. When I got lonely or scared of the dark or sad because one of the girls said something mean, I knew I could crawl into the loft with you, and you would be there for me. Always kind, always with a word—though not always gentle. You protected me. Even later, after Pa made you leave our cabin, you came back over and over. I knew that, if things got too bad, I only had to hide out in the woods until you returned again. Then you would take me with you."

So much emotion clogged Hugh's throat that he couldn't respond. Had Louis really thought of him that way? So many times he'd worried he'd not been what his brother needed. He'd hated that they had to leave the Heinrichs', that Louis had to be subjected to their pa. So many times he'd failed his brother.

Louis didn't seem to mind his silence, just kept talking. "I was actually packing to do exactly that the day you came to tell me you found me a job." Something like pain entered his brother's expression, a look so rare for him. "I just couldn't do it anymore. Couldn't keep trying to smooth things over with Pa. I was done, and I planned to live out in the woods until you came again." The look curved into a sad smile. "And there you were, standing on our doorstep, even bigger than I remembered you. You saved me then just like you had a hundred times before and have a hundred times since."

Hugh managed a smile even as he blinked back tears. He loved this boy more than seemed possible. If only he could be the man Louis thought he was.

Louis reached out and clapped Hugh's upper arm. "Come back to the camp soon. Poppy wants to show you the rocks she brought back for you." He stood and took two steps forward, then turned. "You really should think about marrying Watkuese. I've never seen you as happy as you are around them. And I happen to know you're Poppy's favorite. Heard it straight from the source."

Then he turned and faded into the darkness, leaving Hugh with more questions than he could hope to answer.

CHAPTER 19

$\mathcal{H}$ugh studied his uneven stitches in the bright afternoon light, then tightened the knot once more. This toy would be laughed at by any city dweller who had access to fabric and needle and thread, but it was the best he could do with only fur, buckskin twine, and the point of his knife to make holes for threading.

He tried to examine the stuffed horse through the eyes of a six-year-old Shoshone girl. The rabbit fur was the softest he could ever remember feeling. And at least the outline did look a bit like a horse. Or a buffalo.

Hopefully she could at least feel the love he poured into the project. He was going to miss that girl and her shy smile when she brought a rock or a leaf or a feather to show. He'd kept them all, every one she gave him. Reminders he'd treasure for all his days.

A little girl voice sounded now from the direction of the spring, and soon she and Watkuese rounded the bend in the trail. Watkuese walked with only a small limp, and she listened with a half smile to her daughter's chatter about the baby fish they must have seen in the water.

Watkuese met his gaze as they approached, but she looked away too quickly. Was he giving her mixed signals, kissing her, then leaving so abruptly? He didn't mean to confuse her. He'd simply wanted that one last memory.

She couldn't be his, no matter what Louis said. Even if Hugh wasn't as much like his father as he'd thought, even if he did have a little of his mother in him, White Owl was still the perfect match for her and Pop-pank. Hugh couldn't get in the way of that. He loved her too much to want anything less than the best for her. Even if that wasn't him.

Pop-pank grinned up at him. "Guess what we saw in the stream?"

He couldn't help a smile back. "Come sit and tell me." He tucked the stuffed horse under his leg. He could give it to her after she finished her story.

Instead of settling on the fur beside him, she plopped down on his leg. Then she turned so she could look up at him while she spoke. "I was throwing stones in, and I found a really big rock that was so heavy I had to carry it with both hands." She mimicked a waddling motion with both hands cradling something.

For Hugh's part, he could barely breathe past the emotion clogging his chest. This girl had stolen his heart with the way she opened herself to him. Why did she trust him so?

He managed to nod, and she continued. "When I dropped it in the water, baby fish darted out in every direction." Her fingers spread and swished away from her body to show the actions of the minnows.

He finally managed to clear his throat enough to speak. "I'll bet that was something to see."

She grinned. "Maybe you can go back with me and we'll see them again."

"Maybe." He reached for the horse under his leg. "I've been working on something for you." He held up the horse so it was looking at Pop-pank. "As I was stitching him, I told him about this little girl I know who's so smart and funny and kind. He was excited to hear about you, and he made me promise to introduce you. If you like him, he'd like to be your new friend."

The girl's face shone, and she eased out a finger to stroke the stuffed animal's shoulder. "He would?"

Hugh shifted his index finger to make the horse's head bob. "He says yes, you are exactly the kind of friend he wants."

Her smile spread wider, and she cupped both hands together. "Can I hold him?"

Hugh placed the toy in her palms, then let himself enjoy simply watching her. Pop-pank studied the horse, then stroked its side with her fingers. "It's so soft. Even more than Snowy. What's his name?"

"Well, he wasn't sure. I guess you'll have to give him a name."

She shifted on Hugh's leg to face him more. She regarded him for a long moment. "I think his name must be Snowy."

With the warmth in his chest swelling so tight, he had no idea how he would ever leave this girl. Or her mother.

~

*W*hite Owl had returned last night.

Watkuese should have been happy to see him, but the emotions that roiled inside her were everything but. He'd looked weary but not as exhausted as she would've expected.

Now, after they'd all slept one more night in that camp, they were setting out toward the village's new location. The traveler's words had been right—Twin Elk had moved the village to a small valley tucked beside a river that would provide water through much of the winter. White Owl said they would reach it not long after the sun began to descend in the western sky.

She would be home. Not long ago, that word had summoned

relief. But the healing she'd been seeking for Pop-pank—and for herself—had come during the journey. Much of it from the man who now trudged in front of her horse.

His horse, rather. The mount he'd insisted she and Pop-pank continue riding, even though her ankle had healed.

What would happen when they reached the village? Would Hugh and Louis linger there?

A connection had grown between her and Hugh—that was impossible to deny. But something held him back. She could see it in the way he retreated after each moment of closeness they shared. Would he give in to whatever it was that kept him distant?

If he wanted to leave after they reached the village, would she let him walk away? She'd always gone after what she wanted, but she couldn't bring herself to beg a man to choose her. Not even Hugh.

So could she live with his leaving? She would have to, if that was the choice he made. Somehow, she and Pop-pank would keep going and make a good life. She would find a way.

But she didn't have to think about that now. Maybe when they reached the village, Hugh would take her in his arms and beg her to make them a family. That image eased the coil in her belly and gave her a treasure to dwell on for the final stretch of their journey.

Too soon, columns of smoke rose above the trees ahead. As they rounded a bend in the trail, the sounds of children's voices rang through the winter air. Pop-pank peered around Watkuese's side to see.

The village spread before them, with little ones playing in a small grassy area to the side. Pop-pank wiggled in the saddle behind her. "Look. It's Runs Like a Rabbit and Tall Deer."

The children saw them and stopped their play, sidling forward as though suddenly shy.

Watkuese halted the gelding. "You can go to your friends

and greet them." She helped Pop-pank slide to the ground, then dismounted as she watched her daughter run to the others.

Pop-pank's cheery personality had finally returned, and now she asked questions of her friends and chattered about all the things she'd done across the mountains. Watkuese allowed herself a moment to watch and soak in the smiles. A few men from the village had come out to greet White Owl, and the women would seek her out soon. It would be nice to see them all, but she wasn't quite ready to face her old life.

"Watkuese."

She stiffened at Hugh's voice, especially the distance in his tone. She wasn't ready to face him yet either. But she had to, so she turned his direction.

He stood back a few steps, his expression impossible to read. He was like someone she didn't know.

Desperation surged in her chest. She wanted to close the space between them, tear aside the barrier he'd erected, and kiss him until he promised never to leave.

But she couldn't do that, so she lifted her chin and waited for what he would say.

His throat worked. "We'll unpack your things, then Louis and I will head out."

The world closed in around her, pressing on her chest until she could barely breathe. He was really leaving her. Nothing that had happened between them was enough to make him stay. This connection wasn't strong enough.

She wasn't enough.

She nodded but turned away when moisture stung her eyes. She couldn't say goodbye, not without showing her full weakness. She simply needed to get away from the man.

Moving to the packs, she fumbled with one of the ties. "Say goodbye to Pop-pank while I get our belongings." She managed to get the words out without her voice cracking.

After a moment, he obeyed. She tried to focus on her task, but Louis didn't follow his brother.

Instead, he stepped closer to her, then cleared his throat. "Watkuese, it's been a pleasure to know you and Poppy. Thank you for letting us come along. Hugh…" He paused, maybe trying to find a way to explain his brother's actions.

She wanted desperately to turn and face Louis, to beg him to tell her why Hugh refused to see what might come of this thing between them. What made him run?

Was it her? Perhaps she was too impulsive for him, too head-strong. She would never know for sure unless he changed his mind now.

She nodded for Louis's benefit. "I'm glad you came along. Pop-pank and I both are." She nodded in the direction of her daughter, the direction she refused to look. "Make sure you say goodbye to her. She really loves you. Thank you for all you've done for her."

"I will."

As Louis turned and led his horse toward Pop-pank, the girl's voice rose up to pierce Watkuese's ears. "No! You can't leave. You can't leave us."

Watkuese squeezed her eyes shut against the tears that burned their way out. If only she could close her ears too. This would be as hard for her daughter as for her. She should be there to help the girl through, but she couldn't.

Yet she had to.

Forcing her eyes open, she pulled the last of their bedding off the gelding's back and tossed it on the ground with the rest of their things. Then she turned and made herself walk to Hugh and her daughter.

He was kneeling on the ground in front of Pop-pank, and the girl was shaking her head as she sobbed. Louis stood beside his brother but seemed to be letting Hugh handle things.

A surge of anger sluiced through her. How could Hugh

break such an innocent heart like this? It was one thing to walk away from Watkuese as though they'd never shared something special.

But Pop-pank? If only these two had never traveled with them.

~

*H*e could do nothing to make this better.

Hugh's insides twisted as he straightened and stepped back from Pop-pank. Watkuese wrapped her arms around the girl, sending him a glare.

It wasn't supposed to end like this. They were home. They were safe. It should have been a happy moment for Watkuese and Pop-pank. And soon, he'd be out of the way so they could form the perfect family with White Owl.

Perhaps he shouldn't have chosen to leave the minute they arrived at the outskirts of camp. But watching Pop-pank greet her friends, seeing the villagers trickle out to engulf them all back into their lives, he'd felt he had to step away. A quick breakaway would be best.

White Owl came to Pop-pank's other side and dropped to his haunches. The girl's sobs still hiccupped, but when her uncle tapped her arm, she turned to him.

"I have something for you. Something I was saving until you finally came home." He pulled a bow from his shoulder. "This was your father's. He asked me to teach you how to shoot a bow and arrow. Once we greet our friends, I can show you how to draw the bow. One day you will be a good hunter like your father."

This was Hugh's moment to step back, but he couldn't take his gaze from the girl he'd come to love and the man who wanted so much to be the father in her life. White Owl would do his best by them, that was clear.

Hugh would come back to make sure they were safe and had all they needed. He would see how happy they all were, and that would be enough.

Finally, he managed to back away, then slipped toward the horses. Louis waited there, a grim look on his face. He clearly didn't approve of Hugh's choice, but hopefully he would hold his tongue.

As Hugh settled his reins over his gelding's neck, he glanced back at the scene he'd left. White Owl had scooped Pop-pank into his arms and was carrying her toward the village. She'd stopped crying and was holding the bow.

Her father's bow. One more confirmation Hugh was doing the right thing. White Owl could give her so much Hugh couldn't, especially the link to her deceased parents.

Watkuese was striding toward Hugh, and his belly knotted at the determined look on her face. She meant to have her say, and she deserved to.

No matter how much he didn't want to hear it.

How had he let things come so far that he brought such much pain to people he loved? This was why he always kept himself distant. There was too much pain in loving.

When she reached him, she looked from him to Louis, then back to him. Like a mama wolf snarling at a fox come to eat her pups. "Thank you. Both of you."

Those were the very last words he'd expected to come out of her, and he braced himself for the correction she would add.

"The journey would have been much harder without you. And without your horses." She nodded toward their mounts. Then her manner softened a little. "I hope your trapping this winter gives you everything you wish for."

She finally met his gaze—her look tentative—and it was nearly his undoing.

Everything he wished for was here, and no metal traps could change that. He had to leave before he did something he would regret. But first, he had to make himself say this last important thing.

He swallowed, then forced the words. "White Owl is a good man. I think he will make a good husband for you and father for Pop-pank. Listen to what he says about God too."

Her eyes flashed, her chin lifting. She was preparing to give her opinion on what he'd just said, but he couldn't stay and listen. Not anymore.

He turned away, shoved his foot in the stirrup, and mounted. But as they started out, he allowed himself one final glance back.

Watkuese stood alone where he'd left her, watching him. Even from a distance, she was the most beautiful woman he'd ever seen.

It took everything in him to turn back to the trail and leave.

CHAPTER 20

*I*t took everything in her not to sit down and give in to the tears.

Watkuese squeezed her eyes shut and took in one deep breath after another. Pop-pank needed her. She couldn't break down now. Later, when she was by herself, she would let the tears fall. But not now.

At last, she had enough control of herself to turn and walk into the village. White Owl must've asked one of the others to carry their belongings in, for the packs she'd placed on the ground were gone.

As she entered the camp and made her way among the lodges, she accepted greetings from friends. Yet none of their words penetrated her benumbed mind. Their touches on her arm felt like only the brush of wind.

Her own lodge lay ahead, the pattern of buffalo hides as familiar as the stitching on the moccasins she wore. Twin Elk would have ensured his women took it down in the old village, then set it up again here. He was a good chief to these people, and he'd looked out for her since she first joined the group three winters ago.

When she reached her lodge, no sounds came from inside, though she could see the shadow of movement. She slipped through the door flap and took in the mostly empty space. The grass had not been flattened yet, and her belongings were piled in bundles to one side.

White Owl stood beside them, and her gaze dropped to the sleeping form lying across an unrolled fur.

"She just fell asleep." White owl motioned to his niece. "She is glad to be finally home, I think."

Watkuese nodded, her emotions far too raw to speak.

Pop-pank looked exhausted, and the damp hair around her eyes attested to how much she'd cried. She clutched the stuffed horse Hugh had made for her, and the memory of the tender way he'd given the gift brought a new rush of tears she had to hold back. Pop-pank had rarely set the horse down since then. She might be glad to have reached their home, but if given the choice, would she trade it for Hugh and Louis? Watkuese would never ask her such a thing. It was an impossible decision for a child to make. And it wouldn't matter anyway, Hugh had chosen to leave.

"Watkuese." White Owl stepped toward her, his expression earnest. He stopped an arm's length away. He was tall, this brave, but not as tall as Hugh. His muscle was leaner, his shoulders not quite as broad. "Now that we are home, I wish to make you my wife."

His words jerked her attention up to his face. Was he really asking again?

"I will be a good husband to you. You must know this by now. I will be a good father to Pop-pank." His voice softened. "I will love her as her father did. And I will love you as her father loved her mother."

Watkuese closed her eyes against the pain. This was all too much.

She'd *wanted* to be loved in the way Kamana's husband loved her. But White Owl wasn't the man to do it. She knew it in her heart. He was good and strong and would make a great husband —but not for her. She had to find a way to tell him so he would understand and be done with asking.

She opened her eyes and met his gaze. "I can't."

He spun away before she could speak again, and she cringed against what would surely be anger. He turned back. "It's Hugh, isn't it? The white man." His voice held a hard edge.

Perhaps she shouldn't tell him, but it was the truth. And maybe this was the thing that would stop him from asking.

She nodded.

His eyes turned to flint. "He's gone. And even more, he's not one of us. Don't let your impulsiveness make you do something you'll regret."

She forced herself to ignore that last part. Both of his first points might be true, but neither could stop the love planted so deep in her heart. Nor the pain.

She didn't answer, and White Owl finally looked away. He stared at Pop-pank for a long moment, the rise and fall of her shoulders so peaceful amidst the chaos. Would White Owl pull away from his niece because Watkuese refused to marry him? What would it do to her daughter if she lost both the men important to her at the same time—all three, counting Louis.

Finally, White Owl turned to the lodge opening and strode out. Without another word, he was gone.

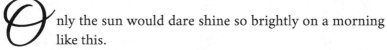

Only the sun would dare shine so brightly on a morning like this.

Watkuese burrowed deeper under her furs and closed her eyes once more. Sand gritted under her eyelids and rocks graveled in her throat. Neither she nor Pop-pank had been fit company after the girl woke from her nap the evening before.

The girl had grumbled and whined, and Watkuese didn't have the energy to do more than prepare a meal and tuck them both in their bedrolls.

She'd heard Pop-pank's tears long after she thought the girl slept, and even though she did her best to soothe with Kimana's song, her own spirit ached so much that she had almost no comfort to give.

Finally in the darkness, when Pop-pank's even breathing promised that she finally slept, Watkuese's tears came.

The loss. The loneliness. The longing.

All of it welled up with a weight so crushing that her entire body ached. She'd fallen asleep somewhere in the midst of it all, and now with morning poking at her like knife blades, she wasn't ready to face the day.

Pop-pank would need food. If Hugh were here, he would have already prepared something warm and hearty.

But he wasn't here, and Watkuese couldn't bring herself to rise until she had to.

The longer she lay there, the more guilt prodded. Pop-pank needed her to be strong now. They were all each other had, and that would have to be enough. They would rise from this pain and make a life they would enjoy. She had to do that. For Pop-pank.

Pushing the covering aside, she worked herself upright and stared around the lodge. She'd not fully unpacked their belongings last night, only pulled out what they needed to use.

Now, packs lay open, their contents spread about. Once she cooked food, she needed to set the place to rights. Make it a real home.

Her gaze moved to Pop-pank's sleeping pallet. The fur covering had been twisted in a wad, which meant her daughter had slept restlessly.

But where was she now?

Watkuese stood, and the familiar ache in her ankle made her

balance wobbly at first. Pop-pank probably only went to relieve herself. Or maybe she sought out White Owl to ask him to teach her to shoot her father's bow as he'd promised. He'd not returned yesterday after the girl awoke, and Watkuese hadn't allowed her to go find him. She had a feeling the brave needed some space from them until his emotions settled.

That had been another source of Pop-pank's ill mood last night, so that was most likely where she was this morning. Especially since the bow was missing from where they'd placed it beside her sleeping pallet.

Watkuese left the lodge and made her way to the edge of the village to take care of her own morning matters. Perhaps she'd find Pop-pank there and wouldn't have to bother White Owl.

But her daughter wasn't among the trees they used for that purpose. So she made her way to his lodge. The door flap hung down, so she called from outside. "White Owl, are you there? Is Pop-pank with you?"

Rustling sounded within, and she waited, doing her best to ignore the tightening in her belly. If only she didn't have to face him so soon.

The flap moved aside and he stepped out. His face held little expression, nor did he speak even a greeting.

"Is Pop-pank here? I think she brought you her bow."

He shook his head. "She's not here."

A ripple of unrest spread through her. "Did she come earlier?" She peered toward the flap but could see little through the cracks on each side. Surely he wouldn't be hiding her daughter from her.

"I haven't seen her at all this day." As if he'd heard her thoughts, he pulled the flap aside and held it for her to look within. He'd not unpacked either, and there definitely wasn't a young girl hiding among the bundles.

She stepped back. "Where is she then?" Even as she spoke the question, her heart realized the truth. But surely Pop-pank wouldn't have gone after Hugh. Both men rode horses, and they would be far away by now. Besides, how would she know which direction they traveled?

"Have you checked with her friends?" White Owl's voice tapped at her thoughts like a buzzing fly. He was right. She needed to search the village first before going after Hugh and Louis. Yet every minute mattered.

She finally met his gaze. "Help me check the lodges. You start on that side of camp and I'll search this way."

Even as she ran to begin asking every person she met, her mind spun to form a plan for how she would find Hugh. She would need a horse. And supplies.

And Someone more powerful to lead her to her daughter.

She couldn't let White Owl come with her this time, not to find Hugh and Louis. But maybe she could beg him to pray.

~

"*I* can't be certain it was him. I only saw him from a distance."

Hugh pulled his rifle from the scabbard where he'd stored it while they dismounted to let the horses drink and rest. He scanned every nuance of the mountain slope where Louis had seen the stranger. Nothing moved, not even the swaying of a bush.

He kept his focus there as he spoke. "The man you saw was wearing the same thing the attacker wore?" What were the chances two men in this wilderness would be dressed the same?

Definitely possible, as vest, shirt, and buckskin leggings were all easily traded for in the forts to the north. But the coincidence seemed too strong.

"Yeah, but like I said, I only got a glimpse." Louis also studied the mountainside. "You think he's been following us this whole time?"

"If it's the same man, I'd say so. At least we're leading him away from the village." One more confirmation Hugh had done the right thing in leaving Watkuese and Pop-pank with her people. A single man wasn't likely to attack an entire Shoshone village. If he wanted vengeance, Hugh and Louis would be much more likely targets.

They needed to tighten their guard though. No matter what, Hugh would not let that murderer hurt Louis.

"We'd better get moving again," Hugh said. "I'd like to draw him farther away from the girls." They'd only ridden a couple hours the night before when Snowy started limping. Hugh would have traveled all night to put more distance between him and the place that caused this aching inside him, but he couldn't force the mare to keep going with an injury. She'd been better this morning, but they'd taken the riding slowly today, stopping often—like now.

They mounted their horses, and Hugh turned his gelding to study the slope once more. Was the man hiding behind a rock watching them? He'd not stolen a gun when he'd escaped, so how would he attack?

A clatter sounded to his left, and he jerked his gaze that way. A rider approached through the pass where the two mountains met. He lifted his gun to his shoulder so he could aim quickly if he needed to.

He didn't recognize the horse, but the rider's coat... His heart lurched and he plunged his heels into his gelding's side.

Watkuese. She'd come after him.

Even though he shouldn't encourage her, if she'd come to ask him to stay with her... His mind leapt from one happy scenario to the next as he closed the distance between them.

Yet as she drew near, her expression held no pleasure. Worry, or maybe even fear, drew her features tight.

His own insides balled into a fist as he reined in beside her. "What's wrong?"

Her horse's sides heaved. "Pop-pank. Has she come to you?" She peered past him as though maybe the girl had been following.

His heartbeat pounded faster. "She's missing?"

Watkuese's voice turned panicky. "When I woke this morning, she was gone. I thought she'd come after you."

Would Pop-pank have attempted that? A young girl on foot? Bile churned in his belly with the thought. They'd covered a lot of rocky territory. A six-year-old surely wouldn't have been able to find them.

"Did she take a horse?" Could she have even caught and mounted a horse on her own? Maybe she had a pony she was accustomed to riding.

"I don't think so." Watkuese turned her mount. "I have to get back. Maybe she went a different direction."

"Wait." Hugh shot a look up the mountain to where Louis had spotted the stranger. He needed to tell Watkuese about the danger. But he hated to add one more worry to her fears.

She paused, waiting for him to speak. Hugh glanced back at Louis, who'd ridden up behind him. "Louis saw someone. Halfway up that mountain." He motioned to the place, then turned his gaze back to Watkuese. "It might be the man who escaped."

She sucked in a breath, her eyes flashing wide. "Do you think he has Pop-pank?"

Louis nudged his horse up beside Hugh's. "I only saw the man, no one with him."

Hugh worked to keep his voice level. Reasonable. "I think he's been following Louis and me. I also don't think he has a gun, or he would have used it already. I want to go with you to search for Pop-pank, but I don't want to draw him back with us."

It seemed an impossible choice. With Pop-pank missing, he couldn't *not* search for her. He'd vowed to keep her and

158

Watkuese safe, and he couldn't leave until he knew she was protected in the village again.

Why had she left to begin with? That question worried him almost more. She'd given him her word not to run away again. Did she think that ended when they reached their destination? Or did she think *he'd* broken his promise, so that allowed her to also?

The ache that had pressed in his chest since he rode away yesterday now twisted tighter. He'd hurt her. He had to make this right. Had to find that sweet little girl.

But he couldn't bring danger with him.

CHAPTER 21

"*I*'ll go after the man." Something in Louis's tone clenched so tight that his voice sounded like a stranger's.

Hugh twisted to face his brother. "You can't go by yourself. He's already proven he's dangerous. I doubt he'd hesitate to kill you if given the chance. He can hide and attack when you ride by. He'll have the upper hand, even without a rifle. You need two people, at least."

His brother eyed him with a look Hugh had never seen before. His eyes darkened. Hardened. As if someone else had taken over his body. "You don't have to protect me this time, Hugh. I'm capable of watching my own back. I'll find the man and do what needs to be done with him. You look for Pop-pank. You might be the only one who can track her, but even more than that, if she's hiding, I think you're the only one she'll come out for."

Louis's words sank over him like a pressing weight, and Hugh closed his eyes as he sorted through all the angles. If Pop-pank had run away because of him—whether she'd come to find him or simply because she was upset—he had to find her. Louis was right. Pop-pank possessed so much talent at hiding, she might never be found unless she came out on her own. And she might not do that unless he was there to beg—and apologize.

He looked to Watkuese, who was regarding him with a wary expression. She couldn't trust him, and though he understood why, that fact twisted the pain inside him even more. He'd left for their own good. He hadn't meant to cause so much hurt.

Turning back to Louis, he nodded. Maybe he could talk some sense into him. "Will you stay here while I'm gone? Snowy's leg could use a rest too."

Louis shook his head. "I'm going up to the place where I saw him. If I can't catch him, I'll at least keep him running so he doesn't follow you."

Hugh had to force himself not to argue. Louis was a man now, though still so inexperienced. "Stay away from rocks he might be hiding behind. And try not to ride through woods or close to trees."

One side of Louis's mouth tipped in a look closer to his usual expression. "Go. I'll come to you in the village in two days. Wait for me there."

Hugh stiffened. He wouldn't sit around while his brother was out in danger. But for now, he nodded. "Be careful."

Then more words pushed up, something he'd never actually spoken to Louis, though he hoped his brother knew it. Still, he had to make sure. His throat closed, but he forced his voice out anyway. "I love you."

Now both sides of Louis's mouth pulled high. "I know. I love you too."

He knew it was time to move on when the tears burned his eyes. Hugh gave a final nod, then turned and nudged his gelding beside Watkuese's mount as they started forward.

They had a little girl to find.

~

*H*ugh patted his gelding's lathered neck as he peered at the ground. They'd been riding hard for a couple hours, and the ground had leveled off, which meant they were nearing the village. Pop-pank might have been able to follow their horses' tracks to this point. Which meant he would be able to find her prints if she'd been at this place.

He could see nothing except hoofprints from when he and Louis had ridden the other direction through here yesterday, and Watkuese's from earlier today. He'd never imagined he'd be traveling the same ground again so soon—with this desperation he could taste.

He had to find Pop-pank. The sun had already passed the noon mark in the sky. What if he didn't find her before night came? Any animals she encountered would frighten her, but the cold would be far worse. And if that attacker followed them back...

Hugh had to clear his mind. Every part of him needed to focus on finding a set of tiny moccasin prints.

There.

He slipped from his gelding's back and crouched beside the winter brown grass. The stalks were crushed in the pattern of a small foot. He turned and searched for another going the direction he and Louis had traveled.

Yes. A second track, then a third. He stayed bent low so he didn't miss a single flattened grass blade as he walked alongside the route the girl had taken.

"You found her trail?" Watkuese's voice held hesitant hope.

"I think so." He hated to build up her expectations in case the tracks ended, but his gut said this was the right path. He'd learned long ago that sometimes a tracker's best tool was his eyes, but other times his instincts might be the only thing worth listening to.

After finding two more prints farther along, he paused to

scan the area around them. They'd been winding along the edge of the tree line, and soon they would reach the rocky ground that began to climb upward. He studied the branches ahead. The girl had already shown herself a good climber. Was she perched in one of them now?

He cupped his hands around his mouth so his voice would carry. "Pop-pank. Can you hear me?"

No sound of a reply. Not even a breeze to rustle the needles of the pine trees. He shifted his focus back to the ground and searched for another track.

As they made slow progress forward, Watkuese took over calling her daughter. The girl never answered, not even a distant cry. With each quarter hour that passed, each time the tracks seemed to disappear, each call of the terrified woman behind him, his fear tightened, churning harder in his belly. What if he couldn't find her? What if he was tracking too slowly? If they didn't reach her before nightfall...

Or if the attacker found her first...

"Are you praying to your God?"

At the sound of Watkuese's voice, his gaze jerked up to her. They'd spoken so little to each other since she first told of Pop-pank disappearing. First, they'd been riding too fast for conversation. But now, the barriers between them loomed so large— not only all the unspoken words from his leaving, but also that cloying fear for Pop-pank's safety.

Watkuese stood a little behind him, watching, waiting for his answer to her question. He straightened as he struggled for the best response. Why did she assume the Almighty was his God? He never spoke of spiritual things, not even with Louis. The way he felt about God didn't seem to be anyone else's business.

But Watkuese... He couldn't keep things from her, not when she asked. Not when his answer seemed important to her.

He had to be honest. "He's not my God. We haven't been close for many years." Speaking those words aloud felt like twisting a knife in his belly. He was the worst kind of rebellious sinner. The type who chose to walk away from the God who'd created the entire world.

Watkuese's brows dipped as a mix of surprise and confusion crossed her face. "Why not? Is he not who White Owl says? A God strong enough to do anything yet who cares about every person He created?"

Every person? *Most* people. God was certainly real, and powerful, and He did care about the people He made. Most of them anyway. The ones who weren't tainted by Pierre Charpentier's bloodline.

But he didn't want to be the one to squelch Watkuese's seedling faith. He couldn't add that to his list of sins. She deserved to become a treasured daughter of the Almighty, she and Pop-pank both.

So he nodded. "He is those things."

Her gaze never wavered from his face. "Then pray to Him for my daughter."

His mouth went impossibly dry, and maybe that was why he couldn't speak. He nodded, then turned back to tracking.

He couldn't deny Watkuese anything she asked, not when it came to finding Pop-pank. And maybe God would answer his prayer this time. For Pop-pank's sake. And Watkuese's.

God, help us find this girl. Keep her safe. And help me not hurt them anymore.

~

*W*atkuese's spirit ached. They needed help.

Though Hugh was the best tracker she knew, that might not be enough. It *wouldn't* be enough. Something inside told her.

They needed help from a stronger power. She'd asked him to pray to his God, the God who White Owl had been certain existed and cared. Hugh had nodded to confirm he would, but why had he said he'd not been close to this Creator Father for many years? What if that stopped his prayers from reaching Him?

She had no idea what should be said in a prayer to this God, but she had to try. Her daughter's life might be at stake.

Creator Father, if You created me as White Owl said, then You know who I am. Watkuese, daughter of Runs Bear of the Nimiipuu tribe. You also know my daughter, and you know how fragile her heart is. Keep her safe. Lead us to her. And heal her pain.

Somehow they had to bandage whatever wounds of grief Hugh's leaving had torn open. But maybe that was something Creator Father could do much better than she could.

Hugh pressed forward as though he could still see Pop-pank's tracks, though Watkuese rarely saw anything except an occasional hoofprint.

The refrain of her prayer repeated over and over in her mind. *Keep her safe. Lead us to her. And heal her pain.* The panic pressing so hard on her chest eased a little, though fear still tingled through her body. Surely they would find Pop-pank soon. If Creator Father was as powerful as White Owl and Hugh said, He would lead them to her.

A cry sounded in the distance, and she strained to hear better. Hugh jerked his head up to stare that way too. The noise didn't sound human, but it definitely rang with distress.

No other noises came.

She kept her voice soft, though she couldn't keep the worry from her tone. "What was that?"

"Maybe a mountain sheep or goat? But I've never heard them make that noise." Hugh also kept his tone quiet and his gaze focused in the distance.

"Should we go see what it is? Maybe Pop-pank heard or saw something and went to find it."

He glanced at the ground. "I hate to lose her tracks while we have daylight." Then he lifted his gaze forward again. "But whatever's out there might be in trouble, and she might be with them."

Which meant Watkuese couldn't stay here strolling slowly as Hugh tracked. She turned to her horse and gathered the reins. "I'm going to ride up there."

Hugh mounted as she did, and they pushed their horses into a jog. The terrain had turned rocky, which made it too dangerous to move faster. And they needed to watch for Pop-pank.

As they rode up a boulder-strewn slope, another noise echoed from ahead and around the side of the hill. This one definitely sounded like one of the mountain animals—a goat maybe, it's squeal panicked.

The terror in the cry resonated within her, and she pressed her horse faster. Her mare surged ahead of Hugh's mount, and her heart pounded faster. *Keep her safe, Creator Father. Don't let her be hurt.*

Maybe Pop-pank wasn't with the goat at all, but it seemed too unusual to be coincidence.

They rounded a boulder, and Watkuese's horse shied at the unexpected sight before them. Watkuese gripped her reins and tugged the mare to a halt.

Pop-pank knelt within a cluster of brush and rocks. Hair was matted over her face, and branches obscured parts of her body. Something else moved within the bushes, but Watkuese couldn't focus on that. Her gaze caught on another figure to the right—the person Pop-pank stared at.

That vest covering a dirty cotton shirt, the buckskin leggings so filthy they looked like he'd worn them for years without washing. And the gnarled face and glittering gray-blue eyes that had appeared in her dreams every night since the attack.

CHAPTER 22

*W*atkuese reached for her knife, but the man already held a tomahawk raised toward Poppank.

Though the weapon was pointed at her daughter, the man sneered at Watkuese and Hugh. "One move and I'll plant this in the girl." He spoke English, but Watkuese had learned enough to understand him clearly.

Numbness sank over her entire body, save for the pulse racing through her neck. She couldn't move. Couldn't risk Poppank's life. Her gaze darted to her daughter. The girl hadn't shifted since Watkuese first spotted her.

What was Hugh doing? She couldn't look his way without moving her head. Did she dare? She couldn't anger this crazed stranger.

What did he want anyway? Revenge for the way he'd been treated? Why had he and the other men attacked to begin with?

He straightened, then motioned at her and Hugh. "Throw your weapons down the mountain. All the way down."

She only had her knife, the blade she carried everywhere.

But Hugh had a rifle and a knife, and maybe another weapon hidden.

Keeping her movements slow and clear, she lifted the strap holding her sheath over her head, then tossed it as far down the slope as she could. She dared a quick glance at Hugh to see that he was doing the same. His gaze was locked on the stranger, his eyes intense.

"What do you want?" Hugh's voice came calm and steady. Nothing like the racing through her chest. "Maybe I can give it to you now."

The man ignored his question. "Get off your horses. Go stand by the girl, but one at a time. You first." He motioned to Watkuese.

She gripped her horse's mane tight to keep her arms from trembling as she leaned forward and slid off. Her knees nearly buckled beneath—not from fear for herself. Not much anyway. This enemy still held the honed blade of his hatchet raised toward Pop-pank. How good was his aim? She couldn't risk testing him.

She had to work hard to keep from running to her daughter, but she managed to stay flat-footed as she walked. When she reached the bushes, she finally had a better view of the other creature tangled in them. A goat stood within, legs spread, mouth open and panting. How long had the animal been here? Pop-pank must have been drawn by its cries and tried to climb in and rescue it.

Her daughter still barely moved, but her gaze had swiveled to stare at Watkuese with terror shining in her wide eyes.

Watkuese's own eyes burned, and her arms longed to reach in and pull her daughter from the tangled branches. To wrap her tight and soothe away the fear. To never let anything hurt her like this again. *Creator Father, help us.*

The man was barking orders again, telling Hugh to come stand with them, but not too close.

Hugh obeyed, and though nearly an arm's length separated them, his solid presence eased through her like a calming blanket. If anything could be done to get them out of the situation, Hugh would do it.

But this might be a battle only Creator Father could win.

Hugh's voice rumbled from beside her, as solid as the man. "What do you want from us? I'll give you all I have. You can do what you want with me. Let the woman and child go."

Once more, their attacker's face twisted into an ugly sneer. "They won't go free, and neither will you. You'll watch them die first, just like I had to watch my brothers die. An eye for an eye, the Good Book says. A life for a life."

His brothers. The other two men who'd died during the attack.

She slid a glance to Hugh. Knowing what drove the stranger to this point made their situation feel hopeless. A man that desperate, who'd watched his brothers die in front of him... Perhaps he could be reasoned with. Or perhaps his thinking had gone beyond all reason.

"I'm sorry your brothers died." Hugh must have had the same thought, for it sounded like he hoped to talk the man into changing his mind. "One of my brothers was killed last year, and I still grieve him. But murdering an innocent woman and child won't bring them back."

"Nothing will. But their blood cries out from the ground, just like Cain and Abel." Anger ground the man's words through his tight jaw. She had no idea whose names he spoke of, but his pain was thick enough to feel.

"That's why I can't let you have my brother either." Another voice sounded from beyond the bushes, this one tight and menacing, yet with a familiar ring.

Their captor spun to face the newcomer. He raised the tomahawk higher even as he stepped back. "Drop your rifle or I'll kill the girl first."

An explosion ripped through the air. The man screamed as a bullet slammed into his body, jerking him back. Then he slumped to the ground in a heap, the tomahawk falling from his grip with a clatter.

Everything happened so fast, she had to blink to bring her thoughts into focus. The newcomer moved into view—Louis.

Hugh jumped into action, stepping around her to wade through the branches toward Pop-pank. The moment Hugh reached the girl, she launched into his arms. He hoisted her up, pulling her out of the brush, then wrapped her in his tight hold.

The pair of them blurred as tears streamed down Watkuese's face. Her daughter was safe. Hugh held her tight, and he wouldn't let anything happen to her. The selfish part of her wanted to be the one Pop-pank clung to, but she could be content with this.

Then Hugh turned to her, and Pop-pank lifted her head from his shoulder. The girl reached out to Watkuese.

Her heart sang as she stepped forward. Hugh opened his arm to bring her into the circle. To close her in.

She wrapped her own arms around each of them, breathing in the scent of safety. Of love.

~

*H*ugh had never felt such intense relief as he did holding his girls. Maybe he had to stop thinking of them as his, but in this moment, they were.

Pop-pank started to wiggle, so he eased his hold on Watkuese to give them both some air. He shot a glance at where Louis was poking through the brush.

"Poor fella. There you go." Louis tugged the goat out from the branches. When the animal finally stood free, it still didn't move. Just remained with its legs spread as though in shock.

Louis stroked its neck, and Pop-pank squirmed again to get

down. Hugh shifted his focus past his brother to the man lying on the ground. Blood had spread across the front of his vest. He looked lifeless. It should be safe for him to set Pop-pank free while he went to check their attacker's body.

As soon as he placed the girl on the ground, she edged toward the goat, reaching out a hand to the animal.

As Hugh stepped around the group, he couldn't help watching them.

Louis continued petting its neck. "Come meet our friend. I think he likes being stroked here." He guided Pop-pank's hand to the thick hair.

Hugh turned his attention to the man on the ground. Perhaps he should grab Louis's gun before approaching. But the stranger's face had already turned nearly gray, and the whites of his eyes showed. He'd seen enough dead men to know the signs.

Still, he reached down and scooped up the tomahawk before stooping by the man's side. Two fingers at his neck confirmed no pulse.

Hugh let himself pause there for a minute. What an awful way to end. Three brothers, just like his own siblings. If they hadn't chosen to attack, they might still be riding together. Trapping or exploring or whatever else they'd chosen to pass their time. Had it really been an addiction to strong drink that drove them down this path?

With his own brothers, that same addiction had taken Rafael. Now only he and Louis were left. And he would do everything he could to make sure neither of them ever touched the stuff again.

He glanced back at Louis, who held the goat while it sniffed Pop-pank's hand. A smile had crept up her face. *Thank you, God, for bringing back her smile.*

Hugh pushed up to his feet and approached the group. Watkuese stood just behind her daughter, as though afraid to let her out of arm's reach. He couldn't blame her.

"I guess we better let this fellow find some food and water. He's thirsty." Louis pulled his hands away and stepped back. The goat stood still for another heartbeat, then wobbled forward. Its legs looked stiff at first, but after a few steps, it trotted down the slope.

They all watched it go, and it seemed to take a bit of the brightness from the air around them.

Finally, Hugh turned back to the group. He needed to talk with Pop-pank, needed to somehow make her understand how sorry he was for hurting her.

He stepped in front of her and dropped to one knee so he could be on her level. "We were so worried about you. Can you tell me why you're up here?"

She slid a glance to Watkuese, then nibbled on her lower lip as she turned back to him. "I was looking for you and Louis. Then I heard the goat and thought you might be here with him. He was stuck so I was trying to untangle him."

As he'd thought. What could he say to help her see that things had to be this way? "Pop-pank, your—" He barely stopped himself from saying *your mother*. "Watkuese needs you. White Owl needs you too. I'm sure he's probably very worried about you still." He couldn't stop himself from glancing at Watkuese, but her expression gave away nothing. He refocused on Pop-pank. "You have to stay with them. They love you a great deal, and they'll make a good life for you."

As he spoke, her jaw jutted out in that stubborn look he'd seen before. When he finished, she shook her head. "I'm not going back unless you come too. You have to be with us. We can be a family." Red rimmed her eyes, and she sucked in a breath that sounded too much like a sob.

His own eyes burned, and emotion clogged his throat. He couldn't do this. He wasn't strong enough to break her heart again.

But he had to. For her sake and for Watkuese. White Owl was the better man for them.

He placed his hands on Pop-pank's arms, willing her to believe him. "This is best for you. It's best for Watkuese too. White Owl will take care of you both. I need to get out of the way so he can do that."

He could feel Watkuese shift, but he kept his focus on the girl.

But then Watkuese's tight voice sounded, drawing their focus to her. "I am so weary of everyone thinking they know what's best for me. My entire life, men think they know what's best for me." Her voice rose with each word as she glared at him. "I have a mind of my own, and I know what I want." She pinched her lips together as though debating what to say next.

It didn't take her long to take on that determined look again. "I happen to agree with Pop-pank. You, Hugh Charpentier, are what's best for me. For both of us, I'd say."

He could only stare at her. Had she actually spoken those words, or had he simply wanted to hear them so badly that he'd imagined her voice?

But that determination on her face was softened by something that looked almost like hope. And maybe a little embarrassment.

He slowly eased up to standing, his gaze locked on Watkuese's face. Could she really mean it? Even if she wanted to choose him, even if she was willing to take on a man who often didn't say the right thing, a man with Pierre Charpentier's blood running through him. Even if she was willing to take the risk... "But... White Owl. He's the better man. I think he'll be good to you."

Watkuese's eyes glistened, her mouth softening. "He's a good man. And I hope he'll be a good friend and a good uncle to Pop-pank. But you are the man my heart has chosen. You are the man Pop-pank and I both want. Will you come back to us?"

His heart thundered and his breaths came so quick that he could barely keep up with them. Could she really choose him? Could he let her?

As he stared at her, her brows rose in a look almost coquettish. Daring him to say no. Daring him to say yes.

Pop-pank must have moved aside, for nothing stood between him and Watkuese now. He stepped forward, closing the distance. He took her arms, like he'd done with Pop-pank. But the feel of her sent a very different reaction through his body. He took in the strength of her expression, her intense beauty that always tightened his chest. "Are you sure?" He had to give her one more chance to change her mind.

She lifted her chin the tiniest bit. "I know my mind and my heart, and they won't change."

So much joy washed through him that he might explode. He couldn't speak, so he leaned down and pressed his mouth to hers, giving her his answer in the best way he knew how.

And he made sure his yes was very, *very* clear.

EPILOGUE

*C*ould Hugh make himself wait until spring, or would God somehow produce a miracle? *I know I shouldn't ask for a miracle, Lord, but this is me asking.*

He stepped out of the lodge where he and Louis had been staying and headed toward the river to sort through his thoughts. He and God had been talking a lot more since Pop-pank's kidnapping a few days before. When he asked a question or sought help from the Almighty, he'd been more than a little surprised at how often he'd felt answers pressed upon his spirit.

It seemed God really did care about the eldest son of Pierre Charpentier. The fact that Watkuese had agreed to marry him was solid proof of that fact.

Which brought him back to the question clouding his mind. He and Watkuese could take part in a Shoshone marriage celebration right away, but he longed to have family around.

He had Louis, of course. And Pop-pank would have her uncle there. But none of Watkuese's family would be here—her parents or brothers or Otskai, her cousin who was like a sister to her.

175

As for his family, it would be nice to have Colette and her little one. He had so few relatives left, he counted every person —even those connected only by his brother's marriage. And even Colette's group of friends who'd taken him in. Though he'd done his best to keep them at arm's length, they were the closest thing he had to friends. It seemed wrong not to include all those people in the celebration of the happiest day of his life.

But with winter coming on, they wouldn't be able to cross the mountains again until spring. Not with an easy passing, anyway.

A figure sitting beside the water drew his attention. White Owl.

Hugh shifted his direction to head toward the man. He'd been meaning to speak with him, and now might be the best time, out here where they could talk without an audience.

When they'd first brought Pop-pank back after the attack, White Owl had taken his niece in his arms and clutched her tight, then spoke a few quiet words. Telling her not to run away again, no doubt. The man really loved his niece, that was clear.

Since then, White Owl had surely heard the news that Hugh and Watkuese were to be married. It had spread quickly through the village quickly.

He had to clear the air with this man. He needed to do everything he could to make sure White Owl stayed a part of their lives.

White Owl appeared to be whittling an arrow, with a stack of a half dozen others lying beside him. He didn't look up as Hugh approached, but he had no doubt the man knew he was there.

Hugh stopped a few steps away and stared out at the river. Not a large body of water, more like a wide creek moving swiftly. He couldn't help remembering the river where they'd nearly lost Pop-pank. But this water came no deeper than his knees. She would be safe here.

How should he start the conversation with White Owl? He should just say exactly what he meant. Surely White Owl would appreciate candor.

He kept his focus on the water as he spoke. "You're a good man." He slid a glance at the brave. "I didn't want to think that when you first found us on the trail, but you proved it over and over. I just want you to know how much I respect you. I'm thankful Pop-pank has you for an uncle. And I'm thankful you know God and can teach her about Him."

White Owl glanced up at him, his gaze measured. "I will tell her what I know of the Creator Father, but I wish it was more. I had little time to learn from the missionaries. You must also speak of Creator Father to my niece. Surely you know Him far better than I do."

Hugh swallowed. "I might know more facts, but I'm just now becoming acquainted with Him. I think maybe this is something she needs from both the men in her life."

White Owl turned to stare out over the water, his manner turning pensive. "I will teach my niece everything I can while I'm here. But I think maybe I won't be in this village much longer."

A weight pressed Hugh's chest. He could understand why White Owl might not want to spend time in this camp for a while. Hugh had experienced the pain of loving Watkuese from a distance, and it was miserable. Perhaps time away would bring healing. *Lord, help him find his place. Send the woman You have planned for him.*

White Owl turned to meet his gaze. "I can see you love them. Take care of them both." The unspoken *...for me* filled the space between them. The man truly did plan to leave. Probably soon. Perhaps he wouldn't be willing to wait until spring to accompany them back to the Nimiipuu camp for a ceremony. Or maybe he'd meet them there.

For now, Hugh held the man's gaze and nodded. "I will."

White Owl gave an answering nod, then dropped his focus back to his arrow and resumed carving.

That was enough for now. They could talk more later. At least their communication had begun. Hopefully in time, he could count this man as a friend.

Hugh turned and started back toward the lodges. Watkuese could decide whether she wanted to marry here or wait until spring when they could celebrate with family and friends. Mayhap she'd choose to do both.

When he reached the first of the lodges, a familiar girlish voice sounded ahead. He slowed as Watkuese and Pop-pank rounded the tipi in front of him.

Pop-pank gave a hop when she saw him. "Hugh! I'm bringing my new bow for my uncle to teach me how to shoot it. Do you want to watch me?" She bounded to his side and pulled the bow from her shoulder to show him. Her enthusiasm brought a smile every time. This girl had been through so much, yet her joy had returned.

He made a show of admiring the bow. "It's strong and will last a long time if you care for it well."

She hugged the treasure to her chest. "I'll take good care of it."

"I see White Owl sitting by the river." Watkuese pointed. "He looks like he's working on the arrows he promised you. You can go to him."

Pop-pank darted that direction, skipping her first few steps before she switched to a run.

Hugh chuckled as he watched her go, and when Watkuese stepped up to his side, he slipped his arm around her waist. She fit so perfectly there, exactly as if she were made for him. That missing rib God had intended from the beginning of time.

He looked over at her, and she met his gaze, her sweet smile stirring something in his chest. This woman completed him, made him believe that together they could be special. The family he'd always longed for but never thought to have.

The family only God could have brought together.

Did you enjoy Hugh and Watkuese's story? I hope so!
Would you take a quick minute to leave a review where you purchased the book?
It doesn't have to be long. Just a sentence or two telling what you liked about the story!

To receive a free book and get updates when new Misty M. Beller books release, go to https://mistymbeller.com/freebook

And here's a peek at the next book in the series (White Owl's story!), *Calm in the Mountain Storm*:

CHAPTER ONE

EARLY WINTER, 1831
FUTURE MONTANA TERRITORY

Chapter One

A body lay sprawled beside a boulder. A man. An Indian man. Fear raced through Lola Cameron, and she gripped the pistol tighter, but didn't raise it to aim. Was he dead?

If the man was alive, she didn't want him to think she meant harm. But she was ready if he sprang up to attack. Did Indian braves play possum?

A groan slipped from him, and he shifted as if trying to escape pain. He was alive, at least, but injured or sick? Or perhaps too much strong drink.

And how did he get up here on the side of this mountain? They'd seen no recent signs of others in the past day. Not since leaving the plains for the low peaks that stretched along the edge of the Rocky Mountains. Did he have friends nearby who would come back for him?

She scanned the length of him, starting with the disheveled black hair that covered much of his face, then over the white feathers tied in his braid, down his buckskin tunic and leggings, all the way to his moccasins.

Her gaze tripped there. What was that dark stain spreading across his lower leg? Blood?

"Lola?"

She jerked at the voice of the man approaching from behind her, then let out a steadying breath and settled her grip on the gun. Mr. VanBuren was supposed to be down the slope helping his son set up camp while she searched for firewood. He must have thought she'd been gone too long and grown worried.

She threw out her other hand to slow his approach, but didn't take her focus from the Indian who'd begun to shift a bit more. "Look." She kept her voice low as she pointed to the stranger. "See his leg?"

Mr. VanBuren halted beside her, his breathing a little heavy from maneuvering the incline. "Who is he?" He spoke as quietly as she'd done.

"I'm not sure. I thought he was dead at first."

"Hey, fellow. Who are you?" Mr. VanBuren called out in a gravelly bark that showed his advanced age.

The Indian didn't answer, nor did he move at first. Then his leg shifted, like he was trying to draw it into himself. She still couldn't tell if his eyes were open, with tendrils of hair splayed over his face.

Another groan drifted from him, not the loud obvious kind like when a person pretended to be hurt. This one came from deep within, a soul-deep sound so guttural it barely reached them. If she were a betting woman, she would stake half their food he was truly injured and not quite conscious.

"Are you hurt?" She spoke loud enough for him to hear clearly across the dozen strides that separated them.

No answer. And no more movement from him. She started forward.

"Wait." Mr. VanBuren grabbed her arm. "Let me go first. Maybe we should call Will up here too. We might need both of us if this is a trap."

She eased her arm out of his hold. "I don't think it's a trap. Walk with me if you like." She motioned him forward even as she stepped out of his reach. She appreciated the source of his worries—concern for her—but she'd been caring for herself most of her life. She knew how to be careful, especially around strange men.

Mr. VanBuren crept along with her as they approached the Indian. When they'd closed half the distance, she could make out more of his face. Including the glistening of sweat and the pale bluish pallor.

And that leg. She still couldn't tell if the dark spot was blood, but it was definitely a liquid that had seeped through his leathers. A foul odor grew stronger the nearer they drew.

She stopped just out of reach of the man. The way his shoulders heaved with each rasping breath made her own chest ache. She'd heard of wounds festering so much they made the person ill, but she'd never seen it herself.

Keeping a sturdy grip on her pistol, she stepped beside him and leaned down to finally swipe that hair from his eyes.

"Don't touch him." Mr. VanBuren tried to grasp her arm again, but she moved too quickly. Just because *he* was afraid didn't mean *she* had to be.

Even before her fingers brushed the Indian's skin, she could feel heat emanating from him. When she cleared hair from his face, dark lashes brushed his cheeks. A bead of sweat trickled down his temple.

She glanced down his body. A knife hung in a sheaf suspended from his neck, and a tomahawk perched at his waist. His hands rested on the ground, not very near his weapons. Every sign pointed to him being too ill to be a threat. Still, it would be wise to move them out of his reach.

After extracting the knife and tomahawk, then tossing them out of reach, she pressed her hand to his brow, both to feel its heat and to make her presence clear if his mind were foggy. "Can you hear me? Are you awake?"

His lashes fluttered as though trying to answer, but they didn't open. His mouth was parted only enough to draw in each hoarse breath.

Her own chest ached with his struggles. This man needed help.

She glanced around the little clearing. The boulder on one side and a few trees blocking the wind from the south and west, this could do for their camp. It would certainly be easier than trying to carry this Indian down the hill to where Will was staking the horses.

She looked up at the man hovering beside her. "Can you yell for Will to bring our supplies up here before he unsaddles the horses? I think we'd better camp in this spot so we can help this man."

"Lola." Hesitation laced Mr. VanBuren's voice.

She worked to keep the frustration from her tone. "We can't leave him to die. We have to at least see what's wrong with him."

"I'm getting Will."

As Mr. VanBuren turned and called through the trees to his son, Lola shifted her attention to the Indian's leg. She needed to see what lay beneath that legging. Maybe removing the moccasin would show her enough, and she wouldn't have to cut the leather.

As she shifted down to his foot, the reality of what she was about to do nearly slapped her. She was touching a perfect stranger. *A man. An Indian.*

And she intended to remove his footwear. Women didn't do such things.

Yet, a glance at his face showed that his eyes remained closed, his breathing still labored. Some situations required letting go of decorum. "I'm going to take off your moccasin. I need to see your wound."

She paused, but he didn't answer. Did that mean it was safe to proceed?

She had to lay her gun across her lap and use both hands to unlace the moccasin. With the leather spread apart, she could already see the dark skin beneath. It held a deep purplish tint. Too dark, even for a native man.

She didn't have to remove the moccasin from his foot, for she could reach the bottom of his legging now. The stained area was in the middle of his calf, and the leather stretched tight around what must be significant swelling. The hem was loose enough that she could ease it upward.

As she did, more skin revealed a thick grayish liquid—the source of the foul stench. Her stomach turned and she had to clamp her mouth shut to keep her stomach's contents intact.

The legging wouldn't raise anymore, not without tugging it across the wound. She reached for the knife she'd strapped to her waist. Even as she examined how best to maneuver the blade to cut the leather without cutting the skin, she had to strain to push away her dizziness.

There seemed no better way than to pull the legging enough to fit the tip of her knife between the leather and the skin. She might bring pain, but it had to be done. If there was any chance to help the man recover, she had to clean the wound and douse it in salve.

She'd just fit the tip of her blade against the buckskin when a sharp voice made her jump.

"Lola, what are you doing?"

She glanced over her shoulder to see Will stomping toward her. He held his rifle with both hands, the stock tucked loosely against his shoulder and the barrel pointed at the Indian.

She braced herself over the Indian. "Don't harm him. He's injured and very sick. I have to cut this legging open to see how bad the wound is." If Will VanBuren injured him even more, she'd give him a taste of his own actions. She'd always gotten along fine with Will before he and his father agreed to accompany her west, but he'd not been especially kind to the other Indians they'd met on the journey so far. Showing too much bluster didn't make friends of anyone.

He stopped beside her, then used his boot to nudge the Indian's shoulder. He must have pushed hard, for the brave groaned another of those heart-wrenching moans.

She shooed Will back. "Can you make camp while I tend him? We're going to stay in this clearing." Usually she helped set things up and handled food preparation, even though she was paying both men to escort her through this wilderness. But they were in this journey together, and she'd never expect another to carry her share of the work.

Just now, however, she had another task that needed her full focus. This Indian's life may well depend on her.

Pain shouted to White Owl, summoning him out of the mist. He didn't want to face the torture, but he couldn't seem to resist its tug.

Little by little, the blackness receded as he moved toward the sliver of light.

Voices sounded around him. Was this one of his spirit dreams? But he'd turned away from those spirits. Did the Creator Father also give visions? He'd had so little time with the missionaries. So many questions he'd not thought to ask.

Flames licked at his leg, and he struggled to pull it from the fire. To stop the searing heat.

The poke of red-hot metal scraped up his leg, and he could no longer hold in his cry. A woman's voice sounded again, and that particular agony ceased.

He tried to hone in on her words, but it took several heartbeats of straining to clear away the buzzing in his ears. He could finally make out the sounds she made, but they didn't form words. Not at first.

The white man's tongue. She wasn't speaking Shoshone. No wonder he'd had trouble understanding her. He knew a little

English, but he didn't have enough energy to decipher her words.

Still, he tried. Forced his mind to find the cadence.

"Sorry…hurts," the voice said.

The light creeping through the slits of his eyelids widened as he forced his eyes open a bit more. A figure hovered over his lower body.

What had happened to him? He struggled to make his thoughts work. Buffalo… His horse had been running beside a bull. He'd drawn his arrow. Hit his mark.

The sensation of flying swept through him, then the pain searing his leg intensified.

Now he remembered. The sharp point of a rock had pierced just above his moccasin. He'd lost his horse that day too, and had turned back toward the mountains on foot.

He glanced around him, but his eyelids wouldn't open wide enough for him to see much. Only enough to know he must be in the mountains now, what with all the rocks and trees around.

He shifted his attention back to the figure. She must be the woman he'd heard before. Then another form joined her.

A man, from the sound of his voice. White Owl should get up. Should find out who these strangers were. Learn whether they be friend or enemy.

But he had no strength. Not even enough to keep his eyes open. His lids drifted shut, and he forced his focus on understanding their words.

The man was speaking now. "…looks bad….cut off….leg."

Surely the man didn't mean what it sounded like. Did they think him dead that they would slice off his limbs?

He worked to gather every bit of strength he had. No matter what, he would show them he was very much alive.

Get CALM IN THE MOUNTAIN STORM at your Favorite Retailer!

ABOUT THE AUTHOR

Misty M. Beller is a *USA Today* bestselling author of romantic mountain stories, set on the 1800s frontier and woven with the truth of God's love.

Raised on a farm and surrounded by family, Misty developed her love for horses, history, and adventure. These days, her husband and children provide fresh adventure every day, keeping her both grounded and crazy.

Misty's passion is to create inspiring Christian fiction infused with the grandeur of the mountains, writing historical romance that displays God's abundant love through the twists and turns in the lives of her characters.

Sharing her stories with readers is a dream come true for Misty. She writes from her country home in South Carolina and escapes to the mountains any chance she gets.

Connect with Misty at www.MistyMBeller.com

ALSO BY MISTY M. BELLER

Call of the Rockies

Freedom in the Mountain Wind

Hope in the Mountain River

Light in the Mountain Sky

Courage in the Mountain Wilderness

Faith in the Mountain Valley

Honor in the Mountain Refuge

Peace in the Mountain Haven

Brides of Laurent

A Warrior's Heart

A Healer's Promise

A Daughter's Courage

Hearts of Montana

Hope's Highest Mountain

Love's Mountain Quest

Faith's Mountain Home

Texas Rancher Trilogy

The Rancher Takes a Cook

The Ranger Takes a Bride

The Rancher Takes a Cowgirl

Wyoming Mountain Tales

A Pony Express Romance

A Rocky Mountain Romance

A Sweetwater River Romance

A Mountain Christmas Romance

The Mountain Series

The Lady and the Mountain Man

The Lady and the Mountain Doctor

The Lady and the Mountain Fire

The Lady and the Mountain Promise

The Lady and the Mountain Call

This Treacherous Journey

This Wilderness Journey

This Freedom Journey (novella)

This Courageous Journey

This Homeward Journey

This Daring Journey

This Healing Journey

CPSIA information can be obtained
at www.ICGtesting.com
Printed in the USA
LVHW051403090322
712905LV00014B/1092